OPERATION EXOCET

The Englishmen's looks were perfectly plain to the Argentinian, their meaning clear. He broke into a frenzied torrent of words, pleading, begging, kneeling up and thrusting his head forward in Smyjo's grip on his collar.

Burnaby caught fragments of words that might mean what they sounded like and probably didn't, that being the trap of foreign languages. He thought Alvilas said something about Exocet, but the pronunciation made it difficult to be sure.

Smyjo let out a whistling breath.

'Exocets,' he said. 'The bastards.'

'Well?'

'This turdhead says they're flying in a fresh supply of super-Exocets, secret deal, super-efficient missiles. They can wipe out the Task Force in one strike!'

ADAM HARDY

STRIKE FORCE FALKLANDS
1

OPERATION EXOCET

Futura
Macdonald & Co
London & Sydney

A Futura Book

First published in Great Britain in 1984
by Futura Publications, a Division of
Macdonald & Co (Publishers) Ltd
London & Sydney

ISBN 0 7088 2489 7

Photoset in North Wales by
Derek Doyle & Associates, Mold, Clwyd
Printed and bound in Great Britain by
Collins, Glasgow

Futura Publications
A Division of
Macdonald & Co (Publishers) Ltd
Maxwell House
74 Worship Street
London EC2A 2EN

A BPCC plc Company

CHAPTER ONE

Low and fast over the South Atlantic the lone Sea King drove on for the coast of Argentina. Foul weather stitched ruffled lines across the grey surface below. Gale force gusts buffeted the helicopter, cutting visibility and shrouding her in an envelope of violence.

Swollen clouds pressed down to the sea and sleeting rain rattled with harsh, riveting menace against the chopper's fuselage. She glimmered like a spectre through the grey veils of rain. As the whirling blades battled to keep her flying, her passengers sat buttoned-up, fully-kitted, weapons carefully selected, explosives lavishly packaged; a tightly-knit bunch of the hardest, toughest, most professional fighting men in the world.

The conditions in the Sea King were familiar to these men. The constant vibration, the shuddering as blasts of gale-force magnitude struck them, the continual, howling noise, the smell of oil and the close confinement of men packed together – all these things were routine. All had been experienced by them before and only the ferocity of South instead of North Atlantic weather held surprises.

The chopper dipped and recovered, her blades scattering a whirling, silver sparkle. Again she lurched. The men sat impassively, not over-tense at the obvious dangers, but not fully relaxed. Some of them had their minds fixed on the job ahead on the mainland; others dwelt on the pleasures of the last leave, their drifting thoughts of carnal pleasures mingling with images of plastic and time fuses; and some tried to think of nothing at all.

The submarine monitoring the helicopter's progress suffered her own problems in the atrocious weather. The periscope kept cutting under. Visibility was foul enough to be classed negative. The submarine commander made up his mind to surface and face the full fury of the gale aloft until his task was accomplished.

Veiled in rain, haloed by her whirling blades, the chopper hurtled past above the submarine. Then she shuddered as though she was trying to slice her way through glue. She dipped. For an instant she struggled to rise and fly on. Above the maniacal howl of the gale her engine note roared out in a pulse of power. For a fraction of a heartbeat she lifted.

Then she hit the sea and was engulfed.

The fuselage rolled onto its side. For an instant the grey flank glimmered wetly through the waves like a harpooned whale. A few thin screams pierced the screech of the wind and the roar of the sea then drowned in the uproar and the harsh rattle of the rain. Then the helicopter vanished.

By the time the submarine reached the area of the catastrophe nothing remained. All that could be done was send the signal.

'Operation Exocet wipe-out. No survivors.'

Tom Burnaby woke to the hand on his shoulder. Wide awake at once, he was aware of the more pronounced movement of his bunk, which indicated that they'd butted into dirty weather. The machine-tainted air pressed in closely around him. The dim light drowned as Sergeant Battersby switched on the overhead.

'The Old Man wants you, sir, at once.'

Burnaby noted the emphasis on the word 'sir', a routine

attempt at discipline they affected before the Navy types. He rolled his legs off the bunk and sat up and tousled his hair.

'Righto, Pugsy. I'm there.'

As he reached for his boots the ship put in a particularly vicious roll. Burnaby held on and cursed and fished around for his boots. He wasn't sure if he'd found his sea legs on the long journey south, but he knew he had cast iron guts, so the antics of the vessel did not disturb him.

Boots and belt on, he picked up his red beret. A rough and ready bunch they might be, but in some things the Old Man was a stickler. As Burnaby crabbed along the passageway he reflected again that he always felt something of a cheat. He should be wearing his blue beret. He'd made the mandatory number of drops, of course, more than the required number; but he'd never dropped into action under a silk parasol. He'd tumbled out of a chopper enough times. But, all the same, the feeling remained.

Every time he jumped he'd tried to imagine what it must have been like, leaping out with flak hosing up and the enemy waiting below to blow him apart, or landing in the middle of nowhere with half the company missing and the containers God knew where, and the bridge to hold or the radar station to be taken out. Well, all that little lot had finished before he'd been born, and now here he was sailing off into a new war, that wasn't really a war at all yet.

'Come in, Tom.'

The Old Man sat at his desk, which had been shoved into a corner, the lamp throwing a brilliance of colour into his dark-red hair, setting deep shadows beside his nose. His hat, with its foreshortened peak, his gloves and stick lay ready to hand. A stickler in these things, the Old Man, who could walk the hairiest of them off their feet, could drink them all under the table, could pick up the hardest sergeant instructor and bend him about like a rubber doll.

The Old Man splashed Teachers into a glass and Burnaby

sat across from the desk, took the glass and held it between his hands. He guessed that his own face, a craggy, hard-nosed, blunt-chinned construction that had broken into many a door and bounced many a knobbly fist, showed more of a questioning look than the Old Man was used to.

'Two things, Tom. But before that I want to ask you a question.'

Burnaby said nothing, did not drink, just waited.

'You know that you were not my first choice. That's neither here nor there. I hand-picked every man in Special Strike Force on the basis of knowledge. I just want to say that you fit in well.'

Burnaby lifted his glass. 'Thank you, sir.'

The reddish eyebrows came down over those eyes of a grey Burnaby had never satisfactorily categorised. They could hold a light of so maniacal an intensity that no one could doubt the determination in this man's character. Major Dan Granville, sometimes and for obvious reasons called the Dirty Old Man, lifted his own glass.

'First thing: Guy's got something wrong with his internal plumbing. I've seen him. His face looks like an old boot and it's the colour of last week's cheese.'

"That's a hell of a blow. He'll be all right?'

'The doc thinks so. But he's got to have proper medical attention, and that means the Task Force.'

Burnaby realised what this meant.

'Do you want me to – ?'

'Yes. That's point one. You're now second-in-command.'

Burnaby nodded and waited.

'Second thing: our mission's changed. First part of the signal is just coming in. Decrypting and all that stuff – that's your department.'

'Not aboard ship.'

'No. I suppose not. Can't say signals were ever my strong suit.'

That was an understatement. Major Dan Granville was one of those soldiers who was slap-bang up to date on every new weapons system, could charm his men into getting themselves killed and glory in the doing of it, knew just about all there was to know, and yet had this interesting lacuna when it came to communications. The lads said it was his Nelson's eye. It was, in all probability, the reason why he was able to swan about with his own hand-picked bunch in Special Strike Force and pick chestnuts out of the fire.

'There's been a foul-up. No details. But our job in the Islands is a non-starter.'

Burnaby stood up.

'I'll get along to the cypher room. That is, if they trust me.'

'Give Andy a shout, will you?'

'Right.'

Sergeant Major Andrew Stubbs chopped off his groan as Burnaby woke him. As Burnaby went out after passing on the message, he imagined that among the short, stiff, brutally cropped hairs on Andy's head a few grey tufts stood out alarmingly. At thirty-six Andy was, apart from the Old Man, the eldest in Special Strike Force. But grey hairs already? No way, as they used to say.

His own short brown hair jammed under the beret, Burnaby went off to the communications centre. He fancied himself a pragmatical, competent, professional soldier, so the Navy way fascinated him. He was met by Lieutenant-Commander Pat Dickson, the furrow permanently between his eyebrows. To a background of clicks and buzzes and the electric smell of communications in the shipboard air, Dickson came out into the corridor holding the signal in his hand. He smiled at Burnaby and said, 'No way.'

'So they do still say it,' commented Burnaby, and at Dickson's pained expression let his own smile twitch the corners of his lips. Not one who believed in a continual, inane, toothpaste smile, Tom Burnaby. He'd overheard a lance-corporal, running scared, say to his oppo that Captain Burnaby could freeze a toaster at six hundred paces.

He and Dickson went along to Granville's cabin together. That S.S.F.'s new second-in-command would be told the contents of the signal immediately had nothing to do with it. Dickson was bound to send or take the signal to Granville, as the Old Man was bound to accept it from the Navy at first hand. Burnaby was not concerned about this. There were ways and ways of doing things, and if he believed in cutting corners, he would only do so when it was the best way. Anything else was plain foolish.

When Dickson had left the Old Man looked up from the opened signal. 'We'll need maps of South Argentina, Tom.' With a courtesy Burnaby respected, Granville did not read the signal out or precis its contents. He handed the message across. Burnaby absorbed it avidly.

'Mission Exocet,' he said, not looking up. 'So we have to take out the Argie's air strike power before they can use it. Looks interesting.'

Then, looking up over the paper, Burnaby said, 'There's nothing here telling us why we have to go in. We're tooled up for the Islands.'

'As a Strike Force, we can handle anything,' began Granville, quickly. The light caught in his reddish hair and glinted. Burnaby shook his head.

'I didn't mean that. I meant – if we're hoicked out to do this, what happened to the chaps who were detailed in the first place?'

For a moment neither man spoke, their minds filled with unpleasant suppositions. Then Granville ended the silence.

'If we don't know we can't worry. It's just a job, a job I've trained S.S.F. to do.' He was interrupted by the arrival of Dickson bearing the second part of the signal. It must have been in and out of decipher at record speed.

This part was copied to another recipient. Burnaby absorbed that first, and knew what was following before he read it. It had been sent also to the commanding officer of one of H.M. submarines.

He spoke slowly. 'Was beginning to wonder how we'd manage to get us all ashore before Christmas if we had to use their Lynx.'

'We'll go in Royal Marine style.'

'Just hope the sub's people aren't too fazed by clandestine ops – '

'Oh, come on, Tom! They've probably landed more clandestines than they've had hot dinners.'

'Your confidence puts my mind at rest.'

Burnaby intended no sarcasm. But the words came out sharply. All the same, Major Dan Granville's confidence was there, solid and real, the powerhouse driving S.S.F. The men in the force had no doubts of Dan, the Dirty Old Man.

Sergeant-Major Andrew Stubbs put his head around the door. 'Guy's sleeping, Major. The doc gave him a dose that'd knock out an elephant.'

'Thank you, Andy. You'd better join us. We're going for a little dive in a submarine.'

'Very good, Major.'

The two parts of the signal were digested. W.O.II Andy Stubbs said, 'I'll get the lads moving at first light. It'll mean re-packing.'

'No problem.'

Well, that was true enough. Just that – Tom Burnaby

caught himself reflecting that the Old Man would ride rough shod over any objections to what he wanted done without bothering about niceties of feelings.

'Tom, you'd better cut along and dig out what maps the Navy has aboard. That'll be Patagonia, Tierra del Fuego, down there. And send the Whizz Kid in, will you.'

'Right, Major.'

Everybody had a nickname, by which he was called and by which everyone knew him. The major was called the Old Man by them all, but not to his face. When you talked to Major Dan Granville, you called him Major. And, anyway, wasn't that a kind of nickname?

Up in the charthouse Burnaby was received by the pilot with no stupid inter-service rivalry. They all had a job to do.

'Tierra del Fuego?' The pilot, a young lieutenant with a desperate attempt at a beard shadowing his lean jaws, pursed up his lips. 'You'll need winter draws on down there.'

'Is it so different from northern Norway, Canada?'

'You'll find out.'

The Type 21 possessed a reasonable supply of charts and maps, and Burnaby settled down to get to grips with the geography. The major was hell on wheels to anyone who couldn't measure up.

A gale front coming in from the south west passed during the night and after a wretched time they broke out into clearer weather. By that time, with the rendezvous with the sub coming up, every man of Strike Force was aware of the situation, was re-packed, kitted-up and ready to go.

A grey dawn, misty and overcast, with the temperature down, though in no way as vicious as it would get, greeted them as they made rendezvous with the submarine. In the seemingly casual, magical way of the Navy these two small vessels met in the misty dawn, finding each other unerringly among the thousands of square miles of empty ocean. Signals chattered. Course and speed matched. The Navy set to to demonstrate its expertise to the pongos as the soldiers buckled down to making the crossing.

Standing on the bridge, Commander Neil Simpson watched the soldiers embarking. As they swung inboard they appeared bulky bundles, with thin legs jerking below and thin arms raking out to haul them along, with the jut of a rifle barrel to break the outline. They looked as though they could have handed themselves along the wire with all the ease of a Tarzan, and done it one-handed, with an extra hundredweight of kit dangling from their boots, if required. Simpson recognised hard, tough men when he saw them.

These men of Strike Force did not rush and jabber. They did things with a methodical speed that ate up problems. Commander Simpson sensed that when all around were panicking, these men would remain calm, not because they did not fully understand the situation, but because they did and knew what each one had to do to rectify that situation – or get killed trying.

He noticed, also, the way in which they looked to their leader, this red-haired, ice-eyed maniac, Major Dan Granville. When the major spoke, when he ordered, things got done.

'Get 'em all stowed away below, Number One,' he said to his first-lieutenant. 'Keep 'em out of the way.'

'Aye aye, sir. I don't think they'll be any problem.'

'No. They've done this before.'

The quietness of these men, their containment, was to Commander Simpson merely superficial. Each was like a wound spring, ready to leap into action at the right moment. Until then they were reticent to outsiders, calm and cool, very professional, and, all too obviously, bloody-minded with it.

Then the wire parted as Noggy was about to swing his boots to the plating of the sub. Lieutenant Noel Oswald Gates, Army Air Corps, simply went slap bang down the steel hull and smash into the sea. The broken wire went scything aft, whistling with death, and laid a slicing, white-smothered stroke into the sea. Noggy went under at once.

Tom Burnaby was the first to strip his kit off, the jaguar pack slamming onto the steel plating. But as he dived he was joined by Trampas and Pugsy. They hit the water and felt the sting and bite of it. Someone hurled a lifebelt. Burnaby whooped up a breath and stuck his head down, plummeting, kicking hard with his feet and then arrowing down. The cold had to be ignored.

Where the hell was Noggy?

He had three or four minutes.

He dived again, searching not desperately but with a demonic passion that wouldn't allow the damn sea to snatch away a comrade.

Where the flaming hell *was* Noggy?

CHAPTER TWO

Tom Burnaby did not search at random. He'd marked the spot where Noggy had disappeared, and from there, allowing for the speed of the vessel, he dived and searched, barely able to see, groping, thinking, shutting out the clawing cold, trusting the Navy to handle the ship evolutions. If that damned great screw sucked him in he'd be mincemeat.

Something bulky and gruesome in the water ahead ... His clawing hands gripped on soggy clothing ... A tremendous effort, a lung-bursting, straining thrust, and he broke surface. Almost immediately Pugsy was there, grasping Noggy from the other side, and then Trampas splashed up, and they had him.

A line snaked down. With blurring speed they tied the rope round Gates and managed a hoarse, water-choked yell, and saw him hoisted away aloft. The hands hauled in with a will. Other lines dropped. The three men, gasping, streaming water, shivering, sprawled on the harsh metal plates, stranded but glowing.

'Get 'em below, sharpish!'

Willing hands guided them across the plating and below where the fug and the oil smell and the canned air met them like the scent of fragrant roses. That water had been *cold*!

Neat rum, hot blankets, warm air, a bunk to lie on and

the doc to prod and pry and eventually to nod and say they might still be alive. The Navy doctor concurred.

Burnaby said, 'You disappointed, Sawbones?'

Sawbones sniffed. Captain Edward Parkes, R.A.M.C., had – perhaps – taken to his sobriquet with less aplomb than the others. He was intense, serious, dark, and a damned good sawbones. Hence his name.

'What about Noggy?'

'He'll recover. He took a nasty whack. But he's out of this little jaunt.'

Burnaby fought back the urge to swear. Noggy Gates was a fine helicopter pilot, but, then, so was Burnaby and two or three of the others. That wasn't the point. What was the point was that Noggy was a member of Strike Force who would not be with them. Burnaby had a strong conviction that they'd need everyone on this one, everyone and his dog.

The Whizz Kid looked in briefly. Although the S.S.N. was of sumptuous size to anyone accustomed to submarines of the diesel-electric variety, the members of Strike Force understood that they were a bloody nuisance to the Navy. They were stuffed away with their monstrous piles of kit and if an inoffensive paratroop boot stuck out for a matelot to trip over, accidents could happen.

Strike Force were not about to forget the criminality of that stupid wire. By snapping it had nearly killed one of them. They took that kind of pointless death hard. Noggy had been whipped off back to the frigate and was being taken care of. They weren't sure yet if his skull was badly fractured, fractured, or whole. They'd find out.

When Lieutenant Christopher Smythe-Jones put his smiling face around the door, raising his eyebrows, Burnaby felt the quick shameful stab of intense feeling. Now had it been Smyjo who'd copped it, Burnaby, hating himself, would have felt very, very differently.

'How's it going, old son?'

'We'll live.'

All the members of Strike Force, personally selected by the major – even if Captain Burnaby was a second choice and in by a third recommendation – worked as a team. They got on with one another. Anything less, any antipathies, rivalries, hatreds, might appear good to psychologists seeking to stimulate aggression and the competitive spirit and the flow of adrenalin; to a team doing a job absolute reliance on everyone else was priority Number One. Yet Burnaby couldn't really stomach Smyjo. That his parent unit happened to belong to the Guards Brigade had nothing to do with it. Hell, the Old Man was from the same outfit, if so august a brigade could be called that. W.O.II Andrew Stubbs was a Coldstreamer, the best there was. No, it was something else about Smyjo that got up Burnaby's nose and, try though he might, he had found no way of overcoming the situation.

Trampas turned over and groaned and said, 'I'm carved out hollow internal, Smyjo. Don't they go in for grog aboard?'

'You've got hollow legs, Trampas. But I'll make a journey and see what there is to be discovered.'

Burnaby felt relief when Smyjo went out. As for Trampas, he fished around in his jaguar pack and brought out a bottle. Most of it was lemonade or ginger, but it warmed him up a treat. As to being called Trampas, well, that was obvious. He just looked like it.

Pugsy, over on the third bunk, said, 'I'll help you out, Trampas.'

With his fair hair in that barbarous crop, his cheerful pugnacious face took on an added ferocity, which tickled Trampas no end even though he'd never admit to it. He thumped the cork in and tossed the bottle across. 'Here.'

The S.S.N. drove smoothly on, deep beneath the surface,

her progress straight and as though she ran on tracks. This was comfort indeed and a far cry from the convulsions of the Type 21 they'd just left.

Pugsy, who sometimes remembered his name was Sergeant Albert Battersby, drank and as he did so he could see himself doing just this, tilting a bottle to his lips and glug-glugging down.

Jonie, still half wearing her nightdress, sat on the bed across from him, pouting at his loudly announced decision to have a drink before any more play. Sitting on a bunk in a submarine deep beneath the South Atlantic, he could close his eyes and see that peach-coloured nightdress, and Jonie's body tantalisingly pressing here and there against the thin material. Her hair tumbled about her naked shoulders and the light from the bedroom's single lamp gleamed beautifully from her hair and shoulders. She had a red mouth, had Jonie, without need of lipstick. Now she pouted at him, and drew back and tucked her legs up.

'You're a fine one! If it's going to be like this when we're married, well, mother will be – '

'Will be my mother-in-law, and that's enough.'

'Come on, darling. You're away far too much – '

'I'm in the Army.'

'I know! By Christ, I know!'

'So I'll be away when we're married, too.'

She fluffed around to make herself more comfortable leaning against the padded bedhead and in so doing revealed more of her delectable self with an unconscious and innocent voluptuousness that made Pugsy catch his breath. He swallowed, and threw the empty bottle on the floor.

'Anyway, I'm glad if you are in the Army you're in a safe job. You mind you keep that job at headquarters with your radio – '

He reached for her, feeling her, feeling himself not

caring about safe jobs and Strike Force. 'It's a wireless set,' he said and tumbled her down onto the bed.

And, so, here he was, at his safe job at headquarters.

The funny thing about that last night before he'd reported in and before anyone knew the balloon had gone up, was the whining, yelping, hand-licking, door-onslaughting behaviour of his lovable idiot dog Sasha. He'd had Sasha since she'd been a puppy and he and the dog were devoted. He'd had to let her into the bedroom that night, and Jonie had squealed and laughed, and Sasha had stuck her tongue out and put her jaws on her paws and stared up with such pleading eyes, that all Pugsy had been able to do was carry on with Jonie. It was all perfect and wonderful, and quite right.

'You've got more than hollow legs, Pugsy,' called Trampas.

'Sure. Here.' Pugsy tossed the bottle back.

Safe job at H.Q.! That was not even good for a laugh. Strike Force as a clandestine organisation maintained various fictions to account for the activities of the personnel. The number of courses they'd been on, of postings to high-flown headquarters, of compassionate leaves and all the rest of the covers, had been large and was now growing enormous.

As the S.S.N. forged on, Tom Burnaby conjured up in his mind some of the problems he would face. Arctic training would prove invaluable but conditions were going to be different. For one thing, the climate of the northern and southern hemispheres was remarkably dissimilar. The Falklands were a law unto themselves when it came to weather. About three hundred and fifty or so miles to the west the coast of South America had been sculpted into a vast arc. The shore line had been eaten away by the sea over the millenia and the inland wastes of rocks and pebbles merged into the beach save at certain points where fertile soil allowed cultivation and farms and livestock ranching. All the way around that arc they could meet with danger.

The airfields and bases they knew about were only half the story. Ushuaia down south in Tierra del Fuego was clearly sited to keep an eye on Chile in the territorial squabbles over the islands and the Beagle Channel. There were Santa Cruz and Lobos and Rio Grande, and Rio Gallegos to monitor the Chilean Punta Arenas to the west. He'd casually said to the Old Man that this job was to prevent the Argies from using their undeniably formidable air power. The Task Force had already suffered from the attentions of the Fuerza Aérea Argentina, and there was nothing at all wrong with the guts of those lads. Their naval counterparts in the Aviación Naval were just as tough and determined, and they were the men who would deliver more Exocets if they were not stopped. Losing *Sheffield* was losing one ship too many, and Strike Force had to get in there sharpish and nobble the rest before they could attack again.

Time was running out on them. The British Task Force had to close in to perform its gunfire tasks; that meant closing the Falklands to bombard targets around Stanley and the airfield, and that meant the Super Etendards could be presented with plenty of targets. The words 'close in' and 'tasks' and 'targets' echoed in Burnaby's mind. He could still feel the ghastly sensation of that ice-cold water lapping about his body and drawing all the heat from him. If he felt tired now, God help him when the major began driving Strike Force on.

When Smyjo came back with a bottle Burnaby turned over and closed his eyes.

Stoker came in to bring the news that was radioed once a day from the operation H.Q. at Northwood in London. In a team composed of officers, N.C.O.s and warrant-officers, the man at the bottom of the pile, equivalent to the latrine wallah and the spud basher, had to be at least a lance-corporal. L/Cpl. Derek Smith was called Stoker, a Londoner with a cheekiness that sat oddly on his vast frame and powerful shoulders.

'Lot of argy-barging at the United Nations,' said Stoker. 'They're chasing their tails.'

'Like swimmers putting a toe into the water,' said Smyjo in his lofty fashion. 'Why don't they just admit there's no sensible solution but to chuck the Argies off? They've asked for what they're going to get.'

Trampas put the bottle down.

'They dropped a clanger if they thought they'd get away with just barging in. If they think they can push people around like that – '

'Their junta is very good at pushing people around.'

'Not Brits, though.'

Burnaby said nothing. On the face of it the whole situation was cut and dried. The Falklands had been invaded and naked aggression had been employed. *Ergo*, the Falklands had to be liberated. Trouble was, there was a whole lot more of the problem below the surface, like an iceberg.

The surgeon lieutenant-commander squeezed in with Sawbones and told them they were fully recovered.

Burnaby said, 'That's nice to know. I wouldn't have realised it myself.'

'The skipper'll get you ashore. Don't fret.'

No polite answer could be made to that, and the men of Strike Force said nothing.

Colour rose in the surgeon lieutenant-commander's face, and he made a muffled excuse and took himself off. As he went he reflected that whatever special group these men belonged to they were an extremely tough collection of individuals.

The surgeon had overlooked one point that the men of Strike Force themselves took for granted. For all their casual talk of the rights and wrongs of the situation in the South Atlantic and the fact that they had to go in and help resist aggression, the real reason they fought was simple – they fought for themselves.

Commander Simpson brought the submarine into a shingly bay under cover of darkness with superb professional skill. For Simpson this was just an aspect of the job, a tricky and exacting part, admittedly; but he handled it in the same way Strike Force handled their role, without too conscious an examination of his part in what had to be done.

The tall fin of the S.S.N. afforded a fine vantage point for observation, and Major Granville joined the naval officers on the bridge. That was not a popular move, but the Old Man could contribute his own expertise to the landing.

The Geminis floated off, tethered in a bunch.

When Strike Force performed a task of this nature there was no need for officers and N.C.O.s to run every which way yelling at them to double up and keep quiet and step lively and jump! These men worked as a team. Any nonsense of parade ground bashing, of ivory-dome orders, was completely inappropriate. They spoke only when necessary, and when they did speak it usually meant there was an immediate emergency.

Stars glittered above, the sea ran deeply, and the shoreline lay dark and mysterious, ready to engulf them.

And, said Tom Burnaby to himself as he hitched his rifle up and went down into the Gemini, this is supposed to be a place smothered in fogs all the time. The smell off the land was quite different from the smell of Africa, which is rich and exotic, smoky and golden, dusty and dangerous. The smell of South America was sharper, more acidic, and just as damned dark and dangerous.

Paddling with smooth, powerful strokes the party

approached the shore. Although intelligence suggested all this stretch of coast was practically deserted, to have used the outboards would have smacked of a recklessness the men of S.S.F. only risked when there was nothing else left to do.

The rubber boats touched the shingle.

The Old Man swung his boots into three inches of water and crunched up the shingle. His disruptive pattern smock blended reasonably with the shadows as he went on up, with Andy and two or three others with him, their weapons unslung, loaded and ready to fire. Burnaby bent to assist Pugsy to lift out the radios. The water made a sloshing sound, all its violence deadened by the headland, and the Geminis bumped gently together. They would be paddled back by the ratings aboard. No evidence could be left for anyone to guess that a British force had landed here.

With his own jaguar pack stuffed full, with pouches and water bottles and kit draped around him, Pugsy loomed enormously, even more so as Burnaby positioned a radio on the sergeant's back. Corporal Lawson carried the other radio. Burnaby stepped ashore. He had just straightened up, quelling a brief, fierce awareness that he was treading on hostile territory, when the first gunshots rang out.

Vivid tongues of orange flame broke across the shingle a couple of hundred yards off. The noise hammered out like a maniacal rock band, and then stopped. The whole shooting match began and ended in less than sixty seconds.

Burnaby was halfway up the shingle, panting and lunging on, his Individual Weapon snouting forward, safety off, when the gunfire died. He stopped. The wind soughed by, the feel of the night closed in on him. Then Andy appeared, supporting the slumped figure of Stoker. Briefly, in muttered anger, the sergeant-major spat it out.

'Bloody Argie patrol. Right out of the blue. We took them out, but they got Stoker.'

Blood gleamed black and evil down Stoker's face.

CHAPTER THREE

They carried Stoker back to the nearest Gemini and put him down with exquisite care.

The sailor, paddle gripped in one shaking hand, said, 'Oh, my God!'

The men of Strike Force said nothing.

The Whizz Kid trotted past draped with the ominous bundles of his trade. Sawbones appeared like a spectre and bent over Stoker.

The doctor spoke calmly to the sailor. 'Get this man back to your submarine as fast as you can. You'd better use your outboard. There's been enough noise already.'

The young sailor, after his first shocked exclamation, found it difficult to speak. He nodded. His eyes gleamed white. No doubt he'd had some stupid idea of romance when he'd blacked up his face in tiger stripes like the others for this trip. His fingers managed to ungrip the paddle. It fell with a clatter.

Nobody bothered to bawl him out. As Sawbones said, if anyone was around to hear – they'd have heard! The outboard started after a struggle and that was a relief. No one had too much faith in the Gemini engines.

Now that there was power available some of the other Gemini crewmen started to attach their towlines.

Tom Burnaby stepped forward. 'Stop that,' he said, his voice like a rip-saw. 'You paddle back. You – ' He pointed his Individual Weapon at the scared sailor crouched over the outboard. 'You take the wounded man back, fast. *Move*!'

No one thought to argue with this maniac. Burnaby knew that the sailors believed implicitly that if they disobeyed him he would gun them down. If it came to it, he probably would. It hadn't come to it, so he dismissed the notion. He kept the weapon pointed – not casually – as the sailor took the Gemini out. She roared off, the sound hideous in the night.

To Sergeant Braxton, Burnaby said, 'Brax, get on up front and find out what the situation is.'

Braxton just said, 'Right,' and doubled across the shingle, his boots going shush-shush-shush.

The rest arranged their kit more comfortably, gripped their weapons, and started off. The remaining Geminis began the paddle back to the S.S.N. Burnaby looked around.

The starlight now looked decidedly unfriendly. To Burnaby, those stars glittered mockingly. The op hadn't even begun yet, and they'd lost three men already. Guy's insides had taken him out, Noggy had fallen and cracked his skull, and now Stoker had taken an Argie bullet. This was not a promising start to Operation Exocet.

The temperature, although low, was not too distracting as yet. No doubt that would worsen as the year rolled on. Cold weather, unpleasant though it was, could be dealt with. The clearness of the night was disconcerting. They'd expected fogs and mists, cover in which to operate. As he marched on, Tom Burnaby wondered what would go wrong with the mission next. Then, annoyed, he thrust that out of his mind. That was defeatism. What happened next must be what Strike Force wanted to happen.

Brax came back with the news that the Old Man had everything under control.

The two parties met, still on the shingle which seemed to extend for miles. Not a light showed anywhere. The wind blew across them, and this was to be a permanent part of their life in the days ahead. Their bulky outlines, with kit bulging all over them, their legs thin and muscled, their berets or caps jammed down, their weaponry ready for instant action, they would present a fearsome appearance to anyone unaware of their true nature, and to those who were aware they *would* be fearsome.

The Old Man was as imperturbable as ever. He needed only to give a few curt marching orders, and they set off. The airfield lay something over an hour and a half away at a reasonable speed. If anyone up ahead had been alerted, and it was unlikely that the small arms fire would have been heard at that distance, they'd find no evidence of the shooting, for that had been buried with reverence before Strike Force set off. Inhuman and heartless they might well be called if anyone knew enough of their existence outside immediate circles. But that would have been a completely erroneous description.

As they marched Burnaby – not for the first time – pondered his dissatisfaction with the weaponry they carried. The major's theory was that they were a team made up of individuals. That was a perfectly fine theory. The members of S.S.F. looked to the major as the fount of all wisdom. What he said was Gospel. For Tom Burnaby – who did not forget that he was a second choice at third recommendation – that idea was generally sound but in need of fine tuning. As in this matter of personal weaponry.

Each man was to be his own fire team. Each man, therefore, within the constraints of a balanced force, carried the weapon of his choice. Uzis, of course, a good supply of those. Some men opted to retain their S.L.R., and no doubt might regret that decision. L/Cpl. Oliver carried the team machine gun, and this was a G.P.M.G., and that was wished on them because the major considered it necessary. No one argued.

Tom Burnaby, given a choice and knowing what he wanted, had hesitated. The new bullpup Personal Weapon, designed for 4.85 mm. ammo might be re-chambered for the standard .223″ round; it still presented to Burnaby a superb weapon, finely balanced, economical, capable of doing damage at fighting ranges, and so short and convenient as to be like an extension of his body. He had not suffered from the expected effects of having cartridges exploding next to his ear. And used in the role of a sophisticated, superior sub-machine gun, it was lethal. When you added to that the incredible quantity of rounds you could carry for the same weight of heavier calibre ammo, he was sold.

He'd used some muscle to make sure that Sgt. Battersby and Cpl. Lawson also took a Personal Weapon, and convincing them had been easy. Stocks were limited, for the weapon was not on general issue, and only a special order had secured them. As for L/Cpl. Taylor, he had given thanks to his own personal gods that he had not been lumbered with another G.P.M.G. It was with L/Cpl. Taylor and the need for a sustained fire – or relatively sustained fire – weapon that Burnaby had hesitated.

In the end he had decided that commonality of ammunition within his signals group was more important, and so L/Cpl. Taylor – Spider Taylor – found himself toting a Light Support Weapon, which was simply a Personal Weapon with a bipod and longer barrel. Spider glowed with pleasure. Burnaby just hoped that he had not made a disastrous mistake.

The wind kept on gnawing away at the marching men and the seemingly endless miles of loose stones stretched away on their left as the sea hissed and rattled on their right. Lobos, their preferred target, lay ahead and when they crested a ridge in the loose rocks they could see lights on the horizon.

Marching on now with the others, Burnaby returned to his worries about the weaponry. He suspected the major's hidden reason, probably a reason completely unknown to himself, for allowing personal choice lay in the odd-looking contraption slung over the major's shoulder. Burnaby hadn't believed in it at first, but the Old Man had allowed him to pick it up and hold it. He certainly had not allowed Burnaby to fire it. On a rifle frame, a Lee Enfield of a certain vintage circa 1917, a completely new firearm had been based. The brand new bore was now .45″, only slightly shortened, and the bolt cut down to chamber pistol ammunition. Powerful and sophisticated infra-red sighting equipment gave excellent night-shooting.

Burnaby was content to allow himself to be completely undecided about the Old Man's fantastical bondouk. If it worked, splendid. If it did not Burnaby and all the others would be there to pitch in and retrieve whatever situation the Old Man had got himself into ...

The idea behind the weapon was obvious enough. But Burnaby considered that there were plenty of more modern weapons to do that job.

The lights ahead beckoned them on. The rain, which was likely to be fitful in this interface between arid and stormy regions, plagued them on and off. Smyjo took a couple of men forward to do a reconnaissance and came back to report that the airfield looked a piece of cake. Then in his infuriatingly casual way, he added, 'Not an aeroplane in sight, though, I'm afraid.'

With his customary instant decision-taking, Major Granville said, 'We've come here to blow up aeroplanes, so we'll wait until there are some to blow up. Scout around for a campsite.'

This was found in a gully where no doubt, long ago, a river had run down to the Atlantic. The men got their ponchos out and set about brewing up. Burnaby went off to find the major.

'Think I'll take a look around, Major.'

'Get the feel of the terrain – very good. Off you go.'

Leaving Pugsy and Lawson with the radios, Burnaby took Spider Taylor and set off into the darkness. He had a couple of hours before dawn.

It was like walking across a billiards table. There was practically no cover worth speaking of. A few erratic clouds drifted across and dimmed the star glitter. He and Spider moved cautiously towards the lights. They shone from the windows of a line of sheds and, more ominously, from lamps sited atop posts around the wire. They saw the silhouettes of sentries passing and dropped flat, watching what was going on.

What was going on, as Smyjo had reported, was nothing. The field simply lay there, shrouded in shadow, illuminated in the most awkward places for a quick raid, and devoid of parked aircraft.

Whispering, Burnaby said, 'Spider. I want to take a look in those sheds – hardly call them hangars.'

'Right.'

If this was exceeding his brief, he wasn't worried. If there were aircraft parked in the sheds, then he wanted to know. That would be one in the eye for Smyjo. Also, if there were no aircraft to blow up, there ought to be fuel and bombs and ammunition.

At the far end of the field the lights and the fence were both less of a challenge. Moving with stealth and speed, they rounded the far corner and hunkered down. Nothing changed.

'Right, Spider. I'm going in.'

'What about – ?'

'Stay here. Report back if I'm blown.'

Spider's face, hard and contained like all their faces, nonetheless expressed his disapproval. Burnaby recognised the risks he was taking, but he had confidence in himself. He just did not believe he would be spotted and captured. If he wasn't, the Major might dress him down. If he was, the Old Man wouldn't be on his back, and he was sure enough of himself to believe he would not jeopardise the mission. He had a story ready.

The wire was merely a link-mesh affair that yielded to an upward tug. Spider made the opening and Burnaby slid under. Crouched over, he padded off between the outer limits of the pools of light.

He reached the back of the nearest in the line of sheds and sank down. Light spilled past the corner. He moved warily along the rear of the shed, looking for a spot where he could observe without being seen.

As always in situations of this kind he found himself automatically monitoring his own behaviour. If he was spotted and the balloon went up there wouldn't be time for indulgences like that. But right now he was aware that he was breathing evenly, that his heart beat normally, that although his throat was dry his hands were not wet.

He reached the third shed along and saw no light pooling past its corner. He started up the narrow alleyway between the sheds. At the end he halted. He dropped down onto his stomach and then stuck his head out just above the ground.

To his right the shed door, open, let out dim light. To his left the shed door must either be closed or there was no light at all. In front two men were just walking past, rifles slung, talking softly. Burnaby could speak Russian and German adequately, knew enough of French to get by, but his Spanish was non-existent.

The two men walked past, heads together, and Burnaby

caught the flare of a match held in cupped hands. The men vanished beyond the edge of the shed. He let his breath out, stood up, ran fleetly to the door, looked in.

A single glance into the dimly lit interior revealed that the shed was empty. The door was only a quarter open, and the metal runners were well-greased. He darted back and hunkered down in darkness, waiting. Nothing moved out on the field.

This time he felt even more exposed as he ran swiftly along to the next shed. The door was closed, but enough of a crack remained for him to peer through.

He drew a shaky breath. He had to chance it. He'd come this far, and to retire now without finishing did not appeal to him. He set himself, took a swift, comprehensive, sweeping look around the airfield, and shone his torch through the shed opening. A swift flashing look – nothing, damn-well nothing! – and he switched off the torch and hared back to his alleyway.

His heart did give a couple of extra thumps as he squatted down. By this time he was convinced that there were no aircraft on Lobos Field. He kept well away from the tower, and what were presumably quarters nearby. He was not in the slightest bit interested in killing people; quite the reverse. He was, on this mission, out to stop people being killed by preventing Exocets from killing them.

A group of low and ominous-looking black humps, barely visible off to one side of the field, were presumably ammunition dumps. They would repay a visit when the time came.

Voices rumbled through the night, growing louder. Calmly, Burnaby waited. The two men walked back, heads together, no doubt fiercely arguing the pros and cons of football or women or the state of their intestines. When they'd gone, Burnaby with his usual careful scrutiny of the surroundings, took off for the fence.

Spider said nothing when Burnaby rejoined. Together, they pulled the link-mesh fencing straight.

The lights dwindled at their backs as they walked carefully over the harsh terrain. When they reached the gully the major stood up, a tall and somehow hawklike figure against the night. Smyjo lounged across.

Burnaby said, 'Not a damned plane in sight.'

'That's right,' said Smyjo, with that infuriatingly patronising inflexion in his voice.

'Nothing in the sheds, either, I'd say.'

'Not in those I looked in,' said Smyjo.

Burnaby yawned.

The major said, 'We roster on guard as routine. Now get your heads down.'

'Right,' said Tom Burnaby, and took himself off feeling as big and clever as a mouse turd.

CHAPTER FOUR

The men of Strike Force knew how to dig into a beach so that from the air no observant eye would guess a group of soldiers was there. If the strewn pebbles slid about too much it became uncomfortable; but comfort and Strike Force were most often complete strangers.

Burnaby flopped out and closed his eyes. But, only marginally tired and still keyed up, he found he couldn't sleep with his accustomed ease. He thought of a variety of fatuous subjects, refused to contemplate Smyjo's enormous triumph which the blighter didn't even know he'd won, and then succumbed and thought of Claire.

Claire. Well, it was funny how coincidences did occur. Maybe it was just tired old Fate having a laugh at his expense. He didn't know. He did know that Claire could easily mean far too much to him.

They'd just come back from running up and down mountains in Wales with what felt like not only a sack of cement on their backs but the cement mixer too. Leave being granted, Burnaby had gone down to see an aunt in a pleasant village in Kent. She had been totally involved in baking her cake for the Church jumble. Burnaby had been hauled off to the sports ground near the Church to be put in the severe charge of a Brownie with pigtails. She told him that he was to sell tickets for the Treasure Hunt. So he trailed around the sports ground, seeing the stalls and the bunting and hearing the band shipped in from a Medway town, and looking at the girls – bigger girls than his bossy Brownie – and casting apprehensive looks at the clouds.

He sold what he thought was a fair proportion of the stack of tickets his Brownie – who said she was Ethel, Maisie's sister – had given him. Then the rain fell.

He took cover smartly in a tent where Ethel found him cowering and cut him to ribbons, profoundly contemptuous of his miserable efforts. She, she said, had sold four books and was well on the way to her fifth. He'd better buck up his ideas, or the Church Fete and Jumble wouldn't raise the money for the mini-van. Humbly, he promised to do better. The vicar, Ethel told him, was determined to have the mini-van before the end of the year. Had she said before Michaelmas it would have fitted perfectly into the atmosphere of the situation.

Ethel darted off, her bare legs splashed with mud, haring through the rain and bearing down on a group of unfortunates who'd just arrived and were looking about in some bewilderment. Most people huddled under cover. Burnaby stood under a tent flap which protruded from a green and orange striped affair containing Madam Ostovska, who would tell you anything if you crossed her palm with silver.

The rich smell of mud began to permeate the air, invigorating and yet soothing, a unique scent and a very different one from some of the stinking mud Burnaby had retched at in his adventures. The cloying scent of Madam Ostovska could not compete against that earthy perfume.

'Cross my palm with silver and I'll tell you your fortune.'

Burnaby turned around. Madam Ostovska, her violently coloured clothes rustling, stood before him. Her voice, through the attempts to sound husky and foreign and mysterious, held a clear ring that attracted him. She wore a scarf ringed with coins – brand new pennies – and her face was walnut brown. The goldfish bowl with a torch bulb inside sitting on the card table draped with a Persian shawl illuminated her face from below. She looked suitably mysterious.

'Why not?'

He pulled out a fifty pence piece and made the ritual cross on the woman's palm. She took the money and placed it in a shoe box at her side.

'Let me see your hand.'

Rain clamoured on the tent roof. Water spouted down from a corner and hit the shreds of grass beyond the rug spread under the table and chair.

'You wish to see the past?'

'I know that. What about the future?'

'You know I'm not allowed – ' she began.

The tent collapsed.

Water, canvas, goldfish bowl, shawls, everything went sprawling down into the mud. Burnaby was smothered by heavy folds of wet cloth. He flailed about and a sharp clear voice said, 'Do you mind? That's my elbow.'

He pushed up, fighting the clinging tent and made a surrogate tent with himself as the central pole. She was on hands and knees, reaching around for the shoe box.

Her scarf with the mint-new pennies was gone. The heavily draped clothes had fallen away. She looked up at him. He felt the shock.

Wide, clear grey eyes, a full mouth and a short straight nose added together to make of her a more than ordinarily pretty girl. She had genuine beauty, and that was always disturbing. The stain on her face did nothing to mar that beauty.

She put the shoe box by his feet, and crawled in closer, letting the collapsed tent flop down behind her, and then sat back. She laughed.

Burnaby realised that he was holding the tent so that the

flap folded by his shoulders and water was cascading down his neck. Her laugh broke the immediate spell her surprising beauty had cast on him.

She looked past him turning her head to one side. He saw the light that was striking in through the opening at his back gleam from her mass of fair hair. The fancy fortune teller's clothes concealed a most functional twin set, of the tea-party kind, and her shoes were of the flat-heeled, no-nonsense variety usually considered dowdy. She wore a small string of pearls.

'I really think that was the last of the Lord God Almighty's judgements,' she said in that clear voice. 'The rain's stopped.'

Burnaby twisted around and hauled the tent away and pushed it back. She stood up. They moved a short distance off, warily, and he noticed that the shoe box was firmly tucked up under her arm, with the lid in place.

They both spoke together, and stopped. She tried again.

'I'm Claire Havisham. You must be Tom Burnaby – '

'Yes. How did you – ?'

She smiled. 'I'm a fortune teller, remember?'

'There are no secrets in villages this size, so I'm told. You know my aunt, of course.'

'No secrets.' She laughed again, and Burnaby wasn't quite sure of the point. But her laugh was pleasant. 'You'll know soon enough, I suppose. The vicar is my father.'

So that was the state of the game after their first meeting, a very far cry from what followed, and yet he could still savour the Englishness of it all, particularly squatting down among harsh stones with the wind howling past and Exocets to blow up. He turned over with great caution and checked the time and then closed his eyes.

Breakfast was Spartan, cold, and yet relished as a necessary stiffener for action to come.

That morning the men of S.S.F. crouched in their hides watching the field and ready to deal with the targets they were presented with. When the pair of Super Etendards screamed in from the south-west, everyone perked up. Here, at last, was what they had come for!

Come night, they'd stroll in and plant a little plastic, prowl around doing whatever damage they could, and then pull out. Job finished. They were constrained not to cause any unnecessary loss of life. Being professionals, they would do whatever was necessary to ensure the success of the operation.

Burnaby was curled in his hide, invisible to any observer a few yards away, let alone anyone scanning the inhospitable terrain from the tower. He was just thinking about Claire when the rumble of high-powered engines brought him and everyone else of Strike Force to quivering alertness.

The pair of Super Etendards hurled down the runway, belching, and hurtled into the air. They were not headed eastwards, but back the way they had come. As they flashed past Burnaby saw them haring along, roaring, long, ugly aircraft with raked, moth-like wings. With two smashing crashes of displaced air they vanished. Burnaby did not swear.

The major called an O group, and they cautiously squirmed among the rocks of the gully, wary for the first sound of engines from any direction.

The sight of the Super Etendards had awoken Burnaby's anger. These were the planes, and the deadly missiles they carried, which had sunk a Royal Navy destroyer. They'd sink more if they weren't stopped. He compared their sleek, onward-thrusting appearance with that of the Harrier. He'd always thought of the Harrier as a cheerful, Dumbo-like aircraft with those two big ears flapping, the genial tubby look and the inquisitive snout out front. They appeared overmatched. With R.N. and R.A.F. pilots, the Harriers would perform feats well past belief; but they might eventually go down before sheer, overpowering weight.

'Well?' demanded the Old Man.

Smyjo, as the intelligence officer, cleared his throat. He put his Sterling Patchett Silenced Gun down and said, 'An exercise, a practice for the real thing.'

'That,' said the major, 'is obvious because they didn't fly out to sea but went back home. But what's the object of the exercise?'

'Practice refuelling, I'd say. The Argies have five Super Etendards and five Exocets, as far as we know. They can't afford to waste even one. And their aircraft are operating at extreme range, even the Super Etendards. They have the ability to refuel from Hercules but this looks easier. They fuel and arm at their station, fly to this forward field, top up and then put in an attack at that much shorter range. It's classic.'

'Classic! It means they're down on the field for practically no time at all!'

'So it would seem.'

'The probability is they're worried about a Vulcan attack. Dispersal, flexibility from field to field, and this topping up at the last minute before making a sortie across the sea is their answer.'

The major glared around the ring of taut faces.

'All right. Here's our answer. We position ourselves, hide up closer in, and the moment those bastards touch down – in!'

The Old Man had said it, and no one of Strike Force doubted that what the Old Man'd said would take place.

Smyjo's terrain map was scrutinised, and the field itself related to the best lines of advance.

'A bloody daylight job,' said Pugsy, without rancour,

when Burnaby briefed his signals team.

Every man had a job to do including working out the best routes in. The lack of rancour exhibited by Pugsy was shared to a greater or lesser extent by the others. Burnaby saw this as clear proof of the influence of Major Granville. The major had said that success demanded they go in by daylight. No doubt most of them hadn't even bothered to consider whether or not another way existed. If the Old Man ordered it, it would be done.

The men of Strike Force were not omni-competent. They were multi-competent.

The rest of the day and most of the night was spent memorising the layout and what had to be done almost without thinking when the time came. They ate, rested, talked and checked over their weapons – quite unnecessarily – again.

Ollie Oliver and his machine gun would now repay the trouble of lugging the thing along. With grim humour the Old Man told Ollie that he was their artillery support.

'You shoot us in and you cover us coming out. Here,' the Old Man stabbed Smyjo's map. 'These twenty millimetre jobs could be nasty if you don't take 'em out. And, here, if the Argies think of using flak against us.'

'I do not think we will need to bother about Roland,' said Smyjo, smugly.

Some of the men smiled at the sally. The French anti-aircraft missile Roland would not be used against ground troops. Burnaby did not.

'Remember, it's the Super Etendards and their Exocets we want. Anything else is buckshee.'

L/Cpl. Oliver went over his G.P.M.G. again. He stroked the thing with stubby fingers. Just his luck to be lumbered with the team M.G.; but he could take a twisted sort of pride from the fact that he'd been chosen because he was very good with a machine gun.

His oppo, Cpl. Thwaite, often kidded him. Thwaite would lift his Armalite up and twiddle it and slap it about, and then mockingly challenge Ollie to copy that. Ollie would just go on polishing up his G.P.M.G., and content himself with dark comments about long range and penetration, and wait until the chips were down.

'And, Punkie,' jibed Thwaite, 'I don't want you shooting me up the seat of the trousers.'

Ollie didn't mind old Thwackers calling him Punkie. But didn't it bring back the memories! Back then around 76–77 when he'd been a weird kid with spiky hair and safety pins and chains and what not he'd believed the world would change because of Punk. He was sure of it. Once you'd heard the Pistols, even Clash, your life couldn't be the same again. This was a protest, a way of saying I'm me. Siouxsie and the Banshees came along and then, well, then he'd slouched off because he fancied jumping out of aeroplanes and wearing wings and the red beret and being a little more than his mates down the pub.

He'd survived training. He'd won his red beret and he'd learned to parachute and he had been part of the maroon machine and there'd been Ireland. And, all the time, somewhere he'd believed that Punk lived, even though it seemed to have died a death.

'You wait,' he'd say to Thwackers, 'You wait 'n' see. Next year, it'll be back. There'll be new groups. It won't die.'

'The Who,' said Thwaite. 'Now that's a *group*.'

'Sure, grand-dad.'

So the men of S.S.F. sweated out the night, and were not afraid to acknowledge that they were frightened of what lay ahead. If training, professionalism and dedication could pull them through, they were safe and dry. But they faced more opposition than those simple virtues could easily overcome, and they knew they were lucky to have the most vital ingredient of all. They were Strike Force, they were led by the major, and they fought for themselves. In this lay their true strength.

Towards dawn they sloped off to their positions close up to the wire, making hides and concealing themselves completely. Each man knew where he was going. They were ready.

The day broke cold and wet, and mist hung about. They waited. The day ticked by. The overcast lifted around noon and shortly after that, away to the south-west, the high-pitched scream of engines broke the quietness.

Riding their shock waves, howling with power, two Super Etendards sliced over the field, circled once, and then landed to roll over to the re-fuelling point.

The men of Strike Force leaped into action.

CHAPTER FIVE

Pugsy and Lawson used their bolt cutters neatly and the fence ripped apart like tissue paper. Burnaby rushed through. Spider slid off to the right and the group hared for their objective. From all directions camouflaged figures raced onto the field.

The Old Man raced on ahead with Andy at his heels. Teams raced for the ammo dump. The first smoke grenades went off.

Smyjo had removed his silencer and the S.M.G. chattered. Men moving out to the still-rolling aircraft toppled and fell. The noise began to mount. A siren started to howl.

Because he was signals, Burnaby's team had been given the task of doing something about the tower. Another team would try to bottle up the nearby quarters.

The Dassault-Breguet naval fighters loomed surprisingly large as the major hared for one and Smyjo the other. The aircraft, trundling into a simple and rapid refuelling operation, were met by a devastating attack by men with tiger-striped faces and camouflage clothing who sprayed bullets as they ran forward. The immediate area around each aircraft was clear.

Working with cool speed Andy with the major and W.O.II Smart with Smyjo attached the plastic. One charge was devoted to the Aerospatiale A.M.39 under the plane's starboard wing. Each Super Etendard carried one Exocet. Each Exocet must have cost upwards of a third of a million pounds.

A 20mm. opened up from the tower and instantly Ollie was on to it. His machine gun rattled out. Into the afternoon air the stink of burnt cordite and the raw throat-catching blast of explosives gave an extra impulse to make a man jump. This was not a practice. This was real.

A grenade smashed through the tower window and exploded inside. More smoke grenades cascaded down before the quarters and the flak positions. Less than two minutes had elapsed since Strike Force had raced onto the field. The major's whistle blew above the uproar. Clear and shrill the retire whistled up. The explosives were fitted, the timers inexorably ticking away the microseconds. Time to go.

Ollie let a long burst off through the smoke in the general direction of the quarters. Even above the racket he heard screams. He hauled up his machine gun and started off, Thwackers covering him with his M.16.

Strike Force had been in, were on their way out, and they left chaos behind them.

Spider hosed a full mag into the smoke in the same direction and then pulled back with Lawson. Pugsy followed. Burnaby reserved his fire, backing off, watching with fascination as tracers arched out of the flak positions and laced all along by the sheds. With a little management the Argies might have been induced to shoot up themselves.

The fence, the opening, shingle under foot, a thick feeling of bile in his throat, running and sliding over the loose stones ... Burnaby followed his team as they made off.

The world went up in a blast that threw him forward. More blasts followed as the fuel in the aircraft exploded.

Burnaby took a single swift look back. The field boiled with smoke, black, white, grey; flames shot up. Ammunition was sparkling like fire crackers.

Strike two Super Etendards.

Strike two Exocets.

He scrambled on over the shingle, making for the rallying point. If the Argie soldiers followed on, a defensive line and front had to be formed. Strike Force were not a rabble of rabbits to be snapped up in a snare.

The whole business had taken practically no time at all. Ruthless speed, in and out, had carried Strike Force through to success. Now they felt absolutely confident that the rest of the operation would follow the same pattern.

Each group individual picked up his equipment and shrugged it on almost in the same combined action. They moved off fast, but with complete, calm control.

Hard, professional, they might feel naked and exposed on the loose scree; they were more like a group of scorpions, stingers aloft, ready to strike without hesitation at any pursuit.

When Burnaby reached the gully they had used to lie up in he found Smyjo cursing luridly away.

'Ruined! Look at it! You don't find quality like that in regimental stores, it's all paid for – and now those damned Argies have ruined it.'

He threw down his mountaineering boot – the left boot. The sole flapped and shredded from the upper. Just how many bullets had struck his boot, Smyjo neither knew nor cared. He was incensed that his expensive mountaineering boots, specially designed, had been ruptured.

'It didn't nick your foot, Smyjo?' W.O.II Smart didn't reveal whatever amusement he may have felt.

Had Smyjo raved on that he could heal a wounded foot but he couldn't repair the destroyed boot, Burnaby would not have been surprised.

'No. But I'll fix them.'

As the others pulled out, Burnaby looked back. Smyjo fished out his spare boots, which were just as splendid as the first pair, and put them on. Then he turned to the clearly enjoyable task of wadding a chunk of plastic down each boot, running a wire between and fusing both pieces of explosive. He put the boots together, arranging them casually. He stood back, cocked his head to one side, his features sharp with satisfaction.

'That'll fix one of the bastards, anyway.'

Burnaby refused to allow himself any comment. Had he been on really friendly terms with Smyjo he might have been able to give his point of view, express his disapproval. But he was aware that this was a simple example of why he couldn't be on friendly terms with the intelligence officer. Anyway, he took weak comfort in the thought there was no time.

They left the gully and pulled out, and the pair of boots sat there, waiting.

The major felt perfect confidence that the field and its occupants had been so badly shaken up that any pursuit was going to take a long time to mount. By that stage of the proceedings Strike Force should be well away and invisible. If they had not found good cover before pursuit caught up with them, they would be in for – as old Sergeant McArdle used to say at Catterick – some quantity of pore lubrication.

Bad weather set in after half an hour or so, gusts of wind bearing stinging rain. They put their heads down and struggled on. At least this muck gave them some cover. Constant vigilance on the backtrail took care of immediate pursuit. But each one of S.S.F. knew that the air would be sizzling with radio signals. Heads would roll because of this one successful raid. And, because of the political situation of Argentina at this time, they might well roll in fact as well as hyperbole.

The shingle became less pronounced and as the wind and

rain lashed at them they began to march through mud. On they went, heads down, slogging along, breathing with the rhythm of their march, on and on. This – this they could do superbly.

The major called a halt and they took a short breather. On the backtrail nothing stirred. Ahead lay wide expanses of nothing, with the settlements spread thinly and the farms mainly devoted to ranching stations whose produce ended up in little square tins.

By the time night fell and brought a genuine darkness they'd reached scrub cover enough to afford them all the protection they would need from prying eyes.

'See if you can raise the sub.' The Old Man flopped down and gave a dramatic shiver. Seeing this, Burnaby realised that the Old Man looked like hell.

Breaking various rules and unwritten codes Major Granville had imposed on Strike Force, Tom Burnaby blurted out, 'You all right, Major?'

Granville's hunched form quivered. He was holding his left shoulder with his right hand, the D.P.M. cloth making it difficult to see in the growing darkness. He stared up at Burnaby. The signals officer felt the shock as the man's face glared up, gaunt and drawn, with eyes feverish and burning.

'You're sick, Major – '

'Get that wireless of yours working, Tom, and call the sub.'

The tone of voice, harsh, authoritarian, belied what the Old Man had been attempting to build up in Strike Force. Numbed, Burnaby swung away to attend to his own job. That was clearly the message the Old Man had intended for him.

He called Pugsy to get the main Scimitar humming and then went across to where Sawbones was fussing with his poncho.

'If you want more pills, Tom, you'll – '

'Have you seen the major?'

Sawbones looked across in the gloom.

'There he is. Should I prescribe a white cane?'

'Then you'd better take a look at him.'

The R.A.M.C. officer said nothing further. He threw his poncho to the ground, snatched up his carrying case by the straps and with it swinging from his fist doubled across. Burnaby just hoped Sawbones could muster enough clout to do something and not be bowled over by rank's more devious privileges.

Burnaby's unexpected elevation to second-in-command meant little in the normal course of events. These men had been trained by the major to act as a team. All Burnaby had to do now was decide who should stand watch and then he could leave it to the rest of them to sort out the rota. He went across to Pugsy and Lawson.

The G.E.C.-Marconi Electronics radio was a sweet job, able to skip at pseudo-random across the frequencies at bewildering speed. Whilst it was unlikely that the local radio services would possess equipment that could make any attempt at all to match frequencies, they'd put out jamming signals with all the power they could muster. It was claimed no one could intercept a Scimitar radio's transmissions, although Burnaby had heard that the British had invented a computer programme to do just that. As for the jamming, the Scimitar skipped from frequency to frequency so fast the jammers just couldn't keep up. Pugsy had the manpack set operating and as Burnaby arrived he looked up and nodded.

Some combat radios hopped over a narrow range; Scimitar hopped over the complete frequency range. Burnaby felt absolute security from any ears attempting to listen in.

The sub answered quickly. Within the framework of

operations there was no need for loquacity. The codeword indicating success went out, followed by the codeword confirming the pick-up.

Satisfied, Burnaby turned away to make a check of the perimeter. If the Old Man was going down with a bug, then his second-in-command would have the lot fall on his shoulders. Not for the first time Burnaby wished he and Smyjo got along – although he was sure that Smyjo had no real understanding of the antipathy Burnaby felt.

Most of the reaction to the attack on Lobos Field had been burned off as the men marched here through the foul weather. Their enthusiasm remained high. As professionals they had expected to do a job, quickly and cleanly, and this they had done. There was no excited yammering. What they wanted to do now was get their heads down.

Before he climbed into his arctic sleeping bag Burnaby checked with Sawbones. Captain Edward Parkes, R.A.M.C., looked up with a disgusted expression on his face.

'The stubborn old ox,' he said.

Burnaby was using a portable Betalight and the faint glow washed over the doctor's face, lending him the appearance of a ghoul.

'Tell me.'

'Took a bullet back at the field. Luckily it didn't break his shoulder blade. I've dealt with it and made him comfortable. The quicker we can get him into the submarine the better.'

'Stubborn,' said Burnaby. 'Pig-headed.'

'Hold on, Tom! The Old Man gets his priorities right. There was no time to hang about back there, we all knew that, he knew that – you know it. I rate his actions as stubbornly stupid from a doctor's viewpoint. From a soldier's – '

'Yes. You're right.'

'They must have tried to follow us up.'

'I hope they don't catch us up – '

'For their sakes?'

'If you like.'

'You're nearly as hard a nut as the major.'

'Get some sleep, Sawbones. We should be moving off and we'll have to carry the major – '

'I don't think so.'

Burnaby knew the answer before the doctor had finished speaking.

'The Old Man will walk out on his own two feet. That's his style.'

'We'll see.'

He closed up the Betalight and took himself off.

When he looked down on the Old Man the major was sleeping. Sawbones must have given him enough knock-out drops to put a regiment to sleep, for Granville was a hyperactive, sleeping on and off and always awake at the most inconvenient times for everyone else.

Burnaby could feel the jumpiness in him. He was restless, with a dissatisfaction that had nothing to do with the Old Man, with Smyjo, with his elevation to second-in-command or with regrets over what had been fated to take place on Lobos Field. Despite his own calm judgements, he felt damned jumpy about the hostile patrols that must be out scouring the countryside for them right now.

He prowled impatiently about, at all times maintaining a low profile, checking up like an inexperienced mother on her newborn babies. Plural. He felt the responsibility for the whole of Strike Force on him.

Some of the men slept, others just lay quietly, and the sentries squatted down in invisibility watching every direction.

Andy said, 'You'd better get some rest.' The sergeant-major was canny enough not to use the word 'sleep'.

Burnaby looked around. In the shrouding darkness a few shapeless humps showed, and they could be anything at all to the prying eyes of a patrol. Nothing more could be done until the time came to move off. A little shut-eye would be the most sensible course. He'd be called up well before the off.

'All right, Andy.'

'Sweet dreams.'

The sough of the night wind was the only answer Andy got as Burnaby crawled off to his sack.

CHAPTER SIX

You didn't expect the men of Strike Force to be saints. A tough bunch of expert fighting men, their recreations were tough too. Burnaby joined in with a zest he did not have to feign, although getting drunk was a fool's pastime and one which displeased him. Nonetheless, he felt he could understand the reasons impelling these men to squander their pay in liquor and to roar and bellow and roll about the floor like pigs.

So when a friend from his signal days before Strike Force announced he was getting married, Burnaby went along for the *de rigueur* night out. The small group of soldiers had been scattered to various appointments and duties. They were all interested in what each one had been up to, and Burnaby's ride with the Paras evoked as much interest as Charlie's stint in the Mid-East and Andrew's posting to Washington and Fred's cushy billet at Horse Guards. Bob Gale was getting married on Sunday and on Saturday night they all insisted on going down to Soho to see the sights and let off enough high spirits to keep them restrained on the big day.

That, at least, was the theory.

Fred said he knew the best strip joint.

'You follow me,' he said, not bothering to wink, 'and I'll show you things you wouldn't believe possible.'

'Strippers?' objected Andrew. 'Washington – '

'All you see is what you've seen before.'

'So we see it all again.'

'It's in the artistry, you see,' said Fred, warmly. He had to prove his position as guide. 'These girls can do things to make your hair stand on end.'

'Hair?'

'Wait and see!'

They were all in a boisterous mood. They wore civilian clothes of an inconspicuous cut and demure style and they acted as almost any bunch of high-spirited young men might act out – as they said – on the spree. Thoughts of bombs and machine gun fire were far from this evening's entertainment. Fred led them into the purple-lit interior of the establishment he referred to as his special rendezvous. A foreign-looking gentleman relieved them of a quantity of money, membership being no problem with Fred among them, and a lady wearing very little between navel and neck served them inferior whisky at superior prices. They sat down in the dimness with a scratched record, or perhaps a creased tape, screeching woefully in the background.

The stage was spotlit and the curtains were drawn. Smoke cloyed the air. The sound of heavy breathing vied with the music. This at last died, wailing, and a fat man stepped up with a smile to introduce the attractions.

Burnaby was forced to admit that these girls had thought of a number of novel ways of removing their clothes. But, when all was said and done, what lay under the clothes was, with some differences in the details, all the same. Much more interesting was a study of the ladies' faces. They smiled, unless they were constrained by cracking whips to frown, and they were painted, and they were blank.

Once a girl had finished her act she'd race off to the broom cupboard they called a dressing room, slap on a top and a skirt and bundle her gear into a bag. Then a smart rush for the door still slipping on flat-heeled sandals and a trot along the street to the next establishment that had hired her talents. There she'd go through her routine, dress, and rush on to the next strip joint.

Well, it was a living.

Some of the acts started off with the performers wearing surprising costumes. Animal trainers were popular, as were nuns and traffic wardens and various other strange outfits to make them look more enticing. One girl came on and tripped in her hurry to catch up with the clock. She wore the severe black coat and trousers of a clergyman, the white collar bearing a tiny cusp of lipstick. Her hair was clearly a wig, long and black, swirling as she moved around. Burnaby looked at her over-painted face with some puzzlement.

Fred said, 'Now she's a beauty.'

The others passed favourable comments, as though the girls were entered on a racing form.

Still Burnaby stared at the girl's face, barely conscious of her gentle actions as the coat and the trousers were removed. The frillies looked odd. When they were discarded what was revealed was decidedly more interesting than anything so far, with the white clerical collar still in place around the girl's neck, Burnaby looked at her face, not believing what he saw. But there could be no doubt about it. It was Claire.

It had to be her. He knew he was not deceived, not by the lighting, by her make-up, by the wig. She was beautiful, she was a vicar's daughter, and she strutted naked about a stage in the spotlight glare. Well, it took all sorts to make up a world.

He found himself foolishly wondering if the clothes were her father's. She was clearly enjoying what she was doing, though she might just be faking enjoyment better than the other girls in this pantomime – she was good enough to deceive him if she was. A girl might take her clothes off in public for a variety of reasons. To earn money doing that was as valid a reason as doing the deed for a dare, or to streak across a rugby pitch, or because the girl was plastered. At least, it was a living – of sorts.

There was no doubt about it, Claire Havisham had a gorgeous body. Burnaby looked at her as she performed her last pirouette and exited and as the music crashed on he sighed, and at once began to work out in his mind the earliest he could make another trip down to the Kent village to see his aunt.

Pugsy nudged him and instantly he was awake in the arctic sleeping bag, not sitting up but aware as the sergeant lay at his side, whispering.

'Something odd going on out there, Tom.'

He swivelled sideways. Clouds blotted out the waning moon. The wind sounded like a pack of ghouls after prey.

'Over there, north. Lights and movement – '

At that instant the crash of gunfire smashed out. Brilliant slashes of light from the north stung his eyes. Machine guns and rifles, by the sound of it, chopping at invisible targets. Soundlessly the men of Strike Force crept around to form a front, covering one another, placing their weapons ready. The gunfire broke into a frenzy of one-sided violence. Most of the fire spat from the right with only occasional responses from the left.

'What the hell's going on?' demanded Lawson of no one in particular.

'They're not ours out there, are they?' Pugsy knew that was not possible, but there had to be some rational explanation for the fire fight.

The distinctive crunch of an exploding grenade and the fan of flame told the watching Strike Force that whoever was slugging it out over there was coming to closer quarters. The din kept up.

'Can't get a decent wink of sleep around here,' grumbled

Trampas. His fair-haired, square-jawed face painted with the ferocious tiger-stripes scowled with a perfectly genuine resentment. 'I've a good mind to go over there and knock their damn-fool heads together.'

Burnaby, conscious of the unwanted weight of responsibility hanging on him, pondered the situation. He did not attempt to imagine what the Major would have done. His first concern was the safety of Strike Force. He must not jeopardise them. All the same, information had to be obtained, and some risk accepted.

'Since you've volunteered, Trampas,' he said in his mildest voice. 'You can take your oppo and check out what's going on.'

'If the bastards won't let me get some sack time in then at least I'll be doing something. Come on, Jock, let's go and tickle their feathers.'

Jock grunted and, as usual, said nothing. He'd said too much back in Glasgow, with a broken bottle, and had found a new life in the army. A short, violent man whose accent was practically incomprehensible to anyone born south of Durham – another reason for his taciturnity – he had formed an unlikely partnership with the exuberantly unrepentant Trampas.

Burnaby said sharply, 'We don't want 'em stirred up, Trampas.'

'Strikes me they're stirred up already.'

So Burnaby had to say words he had felt would be completely unnecessary in S.S.F., words of instruction to another hard professional. Still, they were not orders.

'Just find out what's going on.'

When Trampas and Jock vanished into the darkness Burnaby felt a pang of concern. He quelled that by telling himself it was stupid; these men knew what they were up to. Trampas was always out for mischief – what he called having a giggle – and Jock would as lief bash someone over the head as eat a Sunday dinner. All the same, had it been altogether wise to send out two men on patrol when they could have remained safely hidden? Patrol activity brought you in information. It might also give away what you did not want revealed.

The fighting across the way burst up and died down fitfully. The men of S.S.F. tried to work out who was shooting, and argued about the type of weapons being employed. Anybody within three or four feet would have heard nothing of the discussion.

The general consensus of opinion was that, judging from the rifle fire, the Argies were slugging it out among themselves. Two patrols had tangled. This cheered up Strike Force enormously.

The mini-battle erupted again something like three hundred metres off. It moved back and forth, and more grenades testified to the bitterness of the fight.

The clatter of small arms died momentarily and in that brief silence the sound of truck engines revving up explained the lights observed earlier. Two sets of headlights switched on. Abruptly, with a roseate glow and an immediately following blast of noise one of the trucks exploded.

'Jee-zus!' said Pugsy. 'That did them no good at all.'

'They've got to have sussed out they're shooting at each other by now.' Burnaby propped the binocular/monocular nightsight up comfortably and scanned out ahead. The burning truck blanked off some vectors; but he could make out at that range the small, active figures of men leaping about. The nightsight operated on two 1.5v. dry cells, and they were fresh. The single twist grip focus brought details in just that bit more clearly but there was little to see.

Then the shooting started up again and Burnaby handed the nightsight across to Andy. It only weighed two and a half kilos but if somebody else carried it that was okay by Burnaby.

He reached down and touched the pocket Scimitar. Then he discarded the idea of calling up Trampas and asking him what the hell he was playing at. Individual radios were a grand idea; but they had to be used with caution. Disembodied voices could alert the enemy. And, of course, if he knew Trampas, that reckless maniac would be far too far in. At once, Burnaby regretted sending out the pair of them. But aggressive patrolling was the name of the game, surely?

The second truck ground away in low gear. A tremendous racket burst out, and an automatic weapon added its own staccato to the din.

'There goes a jeep,' said Andy.

Presently, the sergeant-major said, 'They're edging over this way.'

'If that's Trampas … '

'Anybody moseying over here'll be knocked over before they get time to wipe their noses,' said Lawson. He and Spider were all set up and raring to go.

Uneasily, Burnaby took the remark as an indication that no matter how drily professional the lads were, they were getting tense in this unpredictable situation.

Spider had his Light Support Weapon extended on its bipod, the thirty round mag clipped in. He had the hood of his arctic combat jacket over his head and as he peered through the sight he looked extraordinarily menacing. The sight fixed to the L.S.W. was the L.R.S.218 nightsight, lightweight at only one and a quarter kilos, with a magnification of x 3.8, and a shadow graticule and 20:30 second generation intensifier tube. Burnaby felt his fingers gripping his own rifle, hard and edged, and he found himself desperately wishing that Trampas and Jock were safely back.

A long, ripping burst of fire as someone let off a full mag from an Armalite was immediately followed by a jeep's engine revving into top gear. Andy said, 'The jeep's taking off.'

Two more grenade explosions and three deliberate, aimed shots – and that appeared to be the end of the night's entertainment.

'Someone's coming in.' Andy had stuck with his S.L.R., claiming that he understood that rifle the best, and now the sergeant-major readied himself to change from the big nightsight surveillance device to the nightsight clamped to his rifle.

Strike Force hunkered down and waited for Trampas and Jock to come in. Also, they waited to knock off anybody who wasn't Trampas and Jock ...

Burnaby's pocket Scimitar came to life and he stuck the earpiece in. Trampas's voice whispered, 'I'm coming in. With friends.'

'Go,' was all Burnaby replied.

The fitful moonlight, veiled by cloud, revealed the blurred outlines of three people. So Jock and Trampas had caught themselves a prisoner – but Trampas had said friends. Odd.

Sergeant Braxton and Pugsy moved out. Moments later the party came in. Trampas fell down. Brax and Pugsy aimed their weapons at the two shadows who stood uncertainly, waiting. Burnaby, baffled, bent above Trampas.

'Where's Jock?'

Blood shone black across Trampas's forehead. He looked wild, drunk, and his features were pinched.

'The Argies were trying to kill these people. Me and Jock got into the middle of it – '

'Jock. Tell me, Trampas. Jock!'

'He was shot, same as me. I tried.' Trampas struggled to sit up and Sawbones, materialising out of the darkness, gently pressed the man back. 'I tried. But they got Jock.

They took him off in the jeep – he wasn't dead.'

Burnaby sank back on his heels. He felt the pressure in his head.

One of Strike Force had been captured. The ultra-secret mission was blown.

This was disaster.

CHAPTER SEVEN

His reaction was not entirely justified. The Argies knew that they were here well enough by this time. But for all that this news was still disaster. It was a personal disaster for Strike Force.

Burnaby knew that had any real chance existed to prevent the Argies from taking Jock away, Trampas would have taken that chance even if he got himself killed doing it.

'Lie still,' he said. 'Sawbones will – '

'Jock,' said Trampas. He looked shrunken, his fair hair matted with dark blood. 'They took him off – '

Sawbones jerked his head at Burnaby.

'Let me get at him, Tom – '

It was a rebuke.

Burnaby took himself off. As he went he reflected that here was another instance of the way S.S.F. acted as a unit within themselves, with their own integrity. He had not said to the doctor, 'How is he? What's wrong with him? Can you fix him?' Or any of the other inane remarks to be found in inferior movies and books. Sawbones would find out what was wrong, would give the best possible treatment available, and then report in to Burnaby. Q.E.D.

He found Brax and Pugsy and some of the others in a ring around the two Argies.

The clouds persisted and the rain had for a spell turned almost to hail, but it was easing now. The night remained overcast and dark. And the damned wind went on howling like the wailing of Dracula's pets.

Smyjo was gabbling away nineteen to the dozen in his excellent Spanish. As the intelligence officer, Smyjo had every right to question the prisoners. Although 'prisoners' was not really the word. They'd come in with the wounded Trampas, had been helping him along. And they'd been shot at by and shot back at the Argies who'd got Jock.

All the same, Burnaby found himself wishing that Smyjo had waited for him to arrive before beginning.

'What's the score?' he said, a little more peremptory in tone than he intended.

Smyjo's smile gleamed greenly white in a Betalight's glow.

'Hullo, Tom. Glad you got here. Will Trampas make it?'

'Sawbones is looking at him now.'

'These two are dissidents, so they tell me. They were being chased and lost some of their people. The lad is upset. The girl is a much – '

'Girl!'

Smyjo's smile was mocking. Burnaby was sure of it. Downright mocking, without a doubt.

'Girl. She's tough.'

'Show the light.'

The little glass-enclosed Betalight threw its faint, pallid beam over the girl's face. Burnaby felt only an enormous disgust and distress. They could do with having a girl along like they could do with losing Jock.

'Name?'

Smyjo cut in.

'She says she is called Dolores.'

At this the girl looked up. Her hair, dark and shining, was pushed up under a crap-hat. She wore an anorak with an exposed zip, like the Paras, all flash and not overly clever. Her eyes reminded Burnaby of those of a spaniel, not a particularly original comparison, but a pertinent one. She looked exhausted.

'That is not my real name,' she said. She spoke in articulate but heavily accented high school English. 'I got it from the movies.'

Burnaby quite liked that.

'Perhaps you'd better tell us your story.'

She looked down again and let her head droop. Burnaby refused to allow himself to think she looked fragile and pathetic. Smyjo had said she was tough, and he would know.

'There is not much story to tell. My brother was disappeared.' She said 'was disappeared' and Burnaby knew this was no grammatical error. She went on, 'We were students, and the military do not like us. After Peron the country has been ... ' She groped around for the right word, and gave up, and said nothing.

'Yes,' was all Burnaby could think of to say.

'Let's have a look at the lad.'

The young Argentinian lay flat, dead to the world, snoring.

'If he continues to make that disgusting noise give him a sharp prod.'

'He's not damaged. Just all in.'

'You were running from those Argies,' began Burnaby. Then he realised that these two were Argies themselves. He ignored that and went on, 'How many, weapons, where from? Any more of you? You'd better tell it all, Dolores.'

A vicious, final gust of rain slashed across them at that moment, before dying away. That, thankfully, appeared to be the last of the downpour. The wind lessened a trifle too. It was not a night for a dog to be out, but to the men of Strike Force, part of whose training had been on the Brecon Beacons, it was bearable.

She put a hand over her face, and Burnaby wondered if

that was to protect herself from the wind or simply a sign of her understandable distress in this situation. He wished that as well as his Russian and German, he had some Spanish, at least up to his standard in French. The devil was that the Latin languages could trip you up if you thought that by learning one you bought an entry into them all with ease.

'You were speaking of your brother.'

'Si. We are just students. We think. The junta do not – ' Again she hesitated, and said, ' — like that. A Ford Falcon took my brother. So we thought more.'

'Go on, Dolores. I know this is painful. But we have to know.'

'But of course!'

The fierceness of her answer made him flinch.

She said that a group had borrowed a friend's car and run away, disappearing themselves. They had intended to see if the rebels in the north and west could help; and then the junta had embarked on their grandiose idea of invading the Falklands. Here Burnaby listened closely. Dolores indicated that she could see the reasons, but she was far too bitter against the junta and what it stood for to allow anything to interfere. 'If the junta failed, it would be brought down. Perhaps – '

'You'll just get another evil bunch,' said Smyjo.

'Perhaps. But, perhaps, the people will wake up.'

'I hope so,' said Burnaby, briskly. 'Now we have to decide what to do with you.'

'I think Jorge can not walk more.'

'He will if he has to. Your car?'

She spoke firmly. 'Burnt.'

The rest of her friends had been killed in the gunfight. The soldiers had shot them. A grenade Jorge had bought from a friend in the army back in Buenos Aires had blown up one of the soldiers' trucks. There had been at least twenty-five of them. Perhaps more. She was not sure.

She was, as the men of Strike Force could see, practically unconscious.

Sawbones came over to look at the Argentinian lad, Jorge, and Burnaby told him to make sure the girl was all right first. Then he turned to Smyjo.

'You'll have to stay with the Old Man and Sawbones with these two, Smyjo.'

'Oh?'

'I'm going after Jock.'

'Of course. But we don't know where they've taken him. They have transport. It's a bit iffy, Tom.'

Gazing around into the night where the dark clouds indicated that the foul weather would recur, Burnaby was aware of the hopelessness of trying to chase after Jock. Yet he couldn't just sit by and do nothing when a comrade was in danger.

'I know, I know – '

'Better wait 'til it's light – '

'They could be miles away by then.'

'I don't think so. Now they know we're here, they'll be back.'

This was not the way they usually talked in Strike Force. Burnaby was obsessed by the crazy idea that the absence of the Major was responsible for this catastrophe.

'Anyway,' said Smyjo in his elegant, casual, damned patronising way, 'as the Old Man saw fit to name you second-in-command then it's my job to go after Jock. Agreed?'

This was approaching an open argument, which was something Burnaby was not keen to get into. Smyjo was right anyway, confound it. The team knew the job, and each individual member knew his job and Burnaby's role was to stay where he was. He grunted something that might have been, 'We'll see,' and crawled off to look at Granville as Sawbones began to check the Argentinian Jorge.

That wouldn't be his real name, either, surmised Burnaby sourly. These kids seemed to think they were in some kind of tenth-rate spy story. Then he saw the stupidity and petty nature of that thought.

These kids had seen their friends taken away by the secret police, and they'd done something about it. They hadn't waited around to join the 'disappeared' ones. And, now, right here and now, they'd had more friends killed. They were the last. They'd tried to do something to stop the junta. But still Burnaby felt uneasy about them.

Why had they come down to the south-east? It was not particularly hospitable. Ranching stations existed, and maybe they had friends. But these cattle stations were not much like the pampas ranches.

He'd been told that the gauchos of this part of the world were a different proposition from those of the pampas. Burnaby didn't know if this was true or not. What he did know as he looked down sombrely on the sleeping Granville was that it was all down to him now. Damn Smyjo! If they'd had the open kind of relationship shared by everyone else, there'd be none of this extraordinarily irritating friction. And the stumer was that Burnaby, as he had thought before, direly suspected that only he felt this. Smyjo seemed to sail serenely on without a suspicion of Burnaby's true feelings.

He made up his mind. He'd call the sub, have the injured sent aboard, and then he'd take a group and go after Jock. The question would be of selecting the men, for they'd all clamour to go. Naturally.

The cold gnawed at him, but he refused even to acknowledge its existence. He'd been colder than this before. His brain continued to function, his joints remained supple. If he was making a mistake, then it was an honest one.

As an experienced signals officer he had complete faith

in the Scimitar and was convinced no hostiles could eavesdrop. Because of this he could remain in communication with the submarine not on a time-call basis but on the expectation that an operator would be listening out for them at all times.

'Pugsy,' he said, wriggling more comfortably into position next to the sergeant and his set. 'Call up the sub. Tell them we're delivering the injured, but we will be delayed.'

'I'm going, Tom,' said Pugsy. He spoke quietly. He spoke as though any argument would be useless.

'Maybe – '

'Listen,' said Pugsy. 'On training – I remember. A sergeant was bellowing in my ear on a twenty mile with fifty pounds of kit. Another fellow got in front of me and the sergeant yelled in my ear, "He's a Scotty! Are you going to let a Scotty get in front of you! We built a wall to keep them out." '

'That's an old one – '

'Sure, Tom, sure. It made me pick the boots up. But Jock's one of us. So I'm going.'

Burnaby remained silent as Pugsy turned to the set and called out for the submarine. One of us. Well, Burnaby was in fact the new boy. With Guy and Noggy out of it, the options tightened up considerably. The sub came through and Pugsy relayed the signal.

Then he swore.

'They're delayed. Put back the pick up by twenty-four hours.'

'*Great.*'

A quantity of colourful language flowed in the brisk dawn air. The men of Strike Force were not bashful about venting their feelings.

'We find good cover and we dig in and go invisible,' said Burnaby.

Light began to seep wanly back into the world.

The Whizz Kid went past draped in infernal devices and W.O.II Smart and Brax came in to report that they'd found a suitable gully where they could lie up. Strike Force moved off like a gathering of phantoms, like spectres draped with the paraphernalia of war. The gully looked promising. The day brightened.

The wounded were placed carefully at the bottom, well clear of the trickle of water. They were wrapped up warmly. The other men spread out, taking up defence positions, each man looking after himself, then his oppo, and then checking that their defensive positions interlocked with the others. This was all routine.

Inured to lack of sleep and starvation rations, they took the opportunity to brew up and heat a few compo tins so that they could get some nourishment inside them. In this game you ate and slept when you could, knowing that you might not have a chance to enjoy either of those luxuries for some long and goddammed time.

The Argies hit just as Burnaby scooped a spoonful of compo into his mouth. Being a man who abhorred waste and one who valued his grub, Burnaby did not spit the lot out as he leaped into action. He swallowed down with a wince and a shudder.

Gunfire crackled about them and bullets started to hit into the rocky outcrop and the shingle above the gully.

'They've got us sighted,' said Andy. He looked furious.

Once again Burnaby took comfort from his knowledge that there was no need to bellow orders at these men. He did not have to shout out, 'Conserve your ammunition. Only fire when you have a target. Keep your heads down.'

Any individual who needed to be told that would not have got into Strike Force; and if he had he would be dead by now.

Leaning among the shingly rocks Andy fired once.

He made no comment at this stage on his shooting.

Burnaby knew that the Coldstream sergeant-major was most unlikely to miss what he shot at.

Most of the incoming fire originated to the north-east. Over there Ollie and Thwackers held the ring, and every now and again they'd pump out a few shots.

Smyjo, his Sterling still lacking the silencer, slid down beside Burnaby.

'I'd say they're a little shy … '

'If they're used to killing terrorists, this may be different for them. But they're still soldiers.'

'Depends what sort of soldiers.' Smyjo clearly wanted to give his intelligence appreciation. Burnaby let him go on. 'They won't be conscripts. Highly unlikely they're Buzo Tactico. We think they were used to take the marines on East Falklands.'

The Buzo Tactico, who wore black and regarded themselves as super-specialist commandos, something like the Special Boat Squadron, were formidable fighting men.

'Anti-terrorist group, then?'

A light voice at his back did not make Burnaby turn around. Dolores had the sense to keep her head down and to speak softly.

'I think these evil men are the same as those who fought la guerra sucia.'

'The dirty war,' said Smyjo. 'We all thought that finished around 1978.'

'They are sailors, or soldiers, maybe airmen. Each – ' She hesitated, searching for the word, and then said, 'Each organisation has its own Special Squads. They kidnap, torture and kill.'

'We heard about the nuns.'

Her voice sharpened. She spoke with passion.

'Do not think they are the real Argentina! We are a proud people. Yes. But we have suffered. The ordinary person is good – kind and loving – we do not like fighting. We are not different. We are like you. But we do not have a –' Again she hunted her vocabulary. 'A sensible government.'

'Sensible,' said Smyjo, quickly. 'Yes, I like that.'

Trampas, his head bandaged, let rip a snort from where he lay under the outcrop.

'You ask all our unemployed if we've got a sensible government!'

'They *don't* "Disappear" you and torture you and hang or shoot you,' said Smyjo. His voice betrayed attitudes that Burnaby did not wish to allow into Strike Force.

About to say something he suspected would be all wrong, he heard the crackle of small-arms fire crescendo all about them. Spider belted out a sharp cry, 'Here they come.' His machine gun ripped into a shattering blast, echoed by the ring of weapons.

In a welter of gunfire and the hiss and crackle of bullets the Argies charged into Strike Force.

CHAPTER EIGHT

Dark, agile figures raced towards the straggle of rocks where Strike Force lay. The insane racket of machine guns surrounded them as they sprinted in shooting. They flowed in from all points of the compass, but Burnaby's quick scan detected instantly the the main assault was being mounted against the south-west, where Spider and Lawson were set up.

Spider's Light Support Weapon hammered. The noise blended with the racket erupting all around. Yet, clearly over the hubbub, Burnaby heard Spider's yell.

'Lawless! Bung me the snail!'

Lawson left off shooting his own rifle and fished out the drum magazine, fashioned after the round drum magazine the Finns fitted to their Valmet M.78 Light Machine Gun. It did look something like a snail, and no doubt the name was a throwback to the old Luger snail mag. It held ninety-five rounds in the 5.56 mm. ammo, and between them Lawson and Spider had it fitted and the rounds cranking through in no time flat. Lawson – Lawless to his intimates – went back to his own Personal Weapon. The dark figures charging in screeching were falling fast. Hate all this though he might, Burnaby just had to hope they'd all fall before they reached Strike Force. Either that, or be sensible and turn around and run off ...

Perfectly confident that everyone was in the right place

and performing what was necessary, Burnaby applied his concentration to his own weapon's sights and started picking targets. Almost immediately the hostiles to his front and right faded. Spider stopped shooting.

Lawson said, 'There's the last of the buggers,' and pressed his trigger. A shapeless mass flopped over out there and lay still.

Burnaby jumped up and ran across to the east side, where there was still shooting. He slid down in a smother of grit beside W.O.II Smart.

'They've got guts,' commented Smart. He fired. 'And that's let a little daylight into them.'

The crackle of musketry died away as the attack faltered and collapsed. Burnaby gave Smart a thoughtful look. Some folk called Sergeant-Major Arnold Smart sir; they were all left behind in the battalion. One or two in Strike Force jocularly liked to call him Smartarse – only in friendly fun, mind, only friendly fun – and the majority just said Smart or, most often, Smartie.

Then, interrupting Burnaby's imaginings, Smart said, 'They've gone to ground. I'll take a look at the major.'

'Righto,' said Burnaby.

Both the Chinese and the Russians with their cult figures had suffered from what Burnaby suspected was insidiously inflicting Strike Force; them and any other of the emergent countries with figures one could bring to mind.

He had to throw these sombre premonitions off. He suspected that his own feelings, being markedly ambivalent, both helped him to see more clearly and alienated him at the same time. He crawled off, this time without raising a scatter of grit, and checked with the new positions. He had to give it to these men, his comrades; after that little skirmish they weren't hanging around in the same positions – not bloody likely! They took up fresh cover and waited, quietly and with the purposeful and deadly professionalism that made them so feared by anybody who was unlucky enough to cross them and live to regret it.

One of the officers in the submarine, during conversation, had found it necessary to make what he considered the right noises. He'd spoken awkwardly, no doubt giving a credit he felt due – as indeed it was! – impelled to speak by that awed and admiring spirit that acts of extreme bravery aroused. He'd used deliberately archaic language to camouflage his own feelings.

'You chaps put up a jolly good show over that embassy business.'

Burnaby had spoken carefully.

'That wasn't us,' he had said, and turned the talk to Willis and Botham and Co.

The little pieces of the unease in him fell further into place as he reached the gully where the Old Man lay. Men were coming in to see him, having a breather, and then leaving for new positions. No one could be faulted. They were all behaving, as that naval officer would no doubt have said, splendidly. Burnaby eased across.

Sawbones saw him and said, 'We were lucky. Not a single hit.'

'Next time, when they get closer, they'll bung grenades.'

'The Old Man ought to be up and around by then.'

'Oh?'

'He'll be a walking chemist's shop, strapped like a mummy. But you know him.'

The uncomfortable – and treacherous – thought hit Burnaby that perhaps he was getting to know Major Dan Granville too well ...

Burnaby said, 'He may get back up on his feet again; but you're the doctor. You can stop him – '

Sawbones didn't bother to make a disgusted snort or even to laugh.

'You try to stop the major doing what he wants to do, sonnyjim, and your own feet won't touch the ground.'

'Here they come again!'

The sharp call was merely a statement of fact. It could have been shouted by any one of Strike Force; as it happened it was Andy who called. Whoever was running the opposition tried to be clever this time and instead of putting in a dispersed three sixty degree attack he bunched his main force. A small diversionary group of men jumped up and down on the shingle to the west; the main attack came from the east. It did not take a genius to suss the situation.

Burnaby's orders consisted of a single sentence to Pugsy, which was, 'Get off my foot, Pugsy!'

Then Strike Force settled down to the unpleasant task of shooting damn fools who knew nothing, or seemed to know nothing, of this kind of soldiering.

Burnaby's foot had taken a nasty dinting as Pugsy dropped into position. As he joined the line-up against the charging men he was convinced that his bruised foot would be the severest casualty Strike Force would take.

Now, if the Argies had a couple of mortars as back-up ...

Or if there had been more of them ...

Or if the clearing weather had deteriorated again ...

But these three ifs did not apply. In brightening light Strike Force, untroubled by indirect fire, could pick targets and see the rapid dissolution of the charge.

The survivors ran off.

Andy said, 'I think they're used to rushing people who don't fight back.'

'Or who don't have decent weapons and can't shoot straight with those they do have,' amplified Smyjo.

Changing positions, surveying the area all around, checking weapons and ammo, were done automatically. Self-preservation for a trained soldier was as much a part of life as breathing.

The men of Strike Force seemed almost to feel sorry for the Argies, and an outsider, Burnaby surmised, might imagine that feeling originated in S.S.F.'s own lofty professionalism. The outsider would be wrong; but try to get a man of Strike Force to explain!

'There's a white flag.' There was no need for Brax to point.

Three men trudged forward, clad in the standard padded suits, waving a white flag.

Smyjo stood up.

'You, Smyjo,' said Andy, 'are a damn fool!'

'They're civilised people, Andy! Not bloody barbarians!'

'We'll see.'

'Your long service has soured you.'

'Too – bloody – right!'

In the event the white flag was honoured – and, indeed, it would have been churlish to doubt that it would be. But Andy had seen a lot in his service, and was a man whose dislike of taking chances equalled the ferocity with which he kept himself – and those over whom he exercised authority – spotlessly clean. He was quite unrepentant about his caution and his suspicion of bad faith, of dastardly tricks. 'When you've seen the little buggers with grenades tucked up between their legs, boyo, you don't blink too often.'

The Argies started picking up their wounded. The shrieks might have been unnerving, they might have evoked pity. But when the shrieking men had been busily trying to kill your comrades and yourself just before they became casualties it was very hard to feel sympathetic.

In this lull between bouts of murderous intensity, Dolores stood upon the lip of the gully, stretched, and looked about. She saw Burnaby below her.

'Why don't you all stand up and relax?'

'That's all right, miss,' said Pugsy, busily taking off Burnaby's boot.

Who among Strike Force felt it necessary to explain that if they all stood up any idiot could count them?

Sawbones was furious.

'You ought to know better than that! Suppose the bruising was extensive? You'd never have got your boot back on, you cretin!'

He pasted the foot, which wasn't seriously damaged, and Burnaby felt suitably chastened. To any man of Strike Force, his feet and legs were his only means of locomotion, and if they suffered injury he was stranded.

Dolores said, 'My friend's home must be close now. We had,' she paused, and then said, 'calculated we had arrived.' So that was where the Argies had been headed before the attack.

'They don't grow much grass on this muck,' said Pugsy.

'Farther on the climate is different,' Smyjo pointed out, 'and there are very large cattle areas in the flat lands of the valleys. Corned beef country.'

'I thought that was the pampas?'

'That's way up north.'

'So we can expect cowboys,' said Spider. He and Lawson were refilling the snail mag.

'The gauchos use modern equipment these days.'

Burnaby looked at the state of his foot with the paste glistening on it, shook his head, and started to put his boot back on. Smyjo was talking to Dolores, the rapid Spanish flowing like electricity, and he caught the word 'desparecidos' – 'the disappeared ones' – repeated a number of times. Only a few hundred metres off the Argies were toiling back carrying their wounded. They didn't bother with their dead.

The distinctive chop-chop-chopping hum of a helicopter broke into the air. Presently the chopper circled into view and landed some way back.

'That'll be the top man,' said Trampas. He wore his

bandage with an air that could only be described as rakish. The khaki-green bandage might not possess the panache of the white bandage around the forehead of days of old, but it still fitted with Trampas's personality. Burnaby did not wish to carry on the associations – that of the last cartridge for the Martini-Henry and the howling Dervishes or Zulus or whatever frenziedly rushing on behind a hedge of steel.

This business Britain had got herself into now was highly reminiscent of the old colonial wars, Burnaby reflected as he waited. Only this time history would bring in a different verdict. If the politicians didn't sort out a sensible solution pretty quickly, the Task Force would have to put its men ashore, and put its guns where its mouth was. The Falklands had been British before there was any such place as Argentina as a country and the people on the islands were British and wished to remain so, therefore the location of the islands had no great bearing on their ownership. If the Argies thought they could steal someone else's property by waving guns and trundling A.P.C.s about, invading peaceful lands, and succeed by naked aggression they had, as they would find out, another think coming.

At this moment though all the fine theorizing did not help Strike Force. They were pinned down, which was unhealthy. Burnaby was torn between wanting the weather to close in and wanting it to remain clear. If it stayed fine they could see the attacks coming in and break them up. Grenades were going to be a problem; but he felt convinced the Argies were short of men out there. He also wanted the weather to close right in, to become extremely murky, for night to come, so he could go out and try to rescue Jock.

He began to play around with the idea that perhaps two or three chaps could sneak out now.

'White flag,' called Andy.

Burnaby peered across the gully lip.

This time the three men with the white flag were preceded by a bulkier figure wearing heavy protective clothing that, whilst perfectly sensible right down south, was overdoing it for this latitude.

'Bloody narner,' said Trampas. His wound was irritating him. He felt like jumping up and, white flag or no damned white flag, grabbing hold of this poofter and belting him and shouting, 'Where's Jock? What have you done with my oppo?'

What was the point of all this, anyway? Sure, Strike Force was a good mob to be in, the very best there was, stemming from the parent unit all according to rules and regulations. But a few stinking little islands stuck away down at the bottom of the world with sheep and sod-all else. So the folk were British. So was Jock. Let 'em come back to Britain and give the sodding islands to the stinking Argies. If anything had happened to Jock Trampas wouldn't answer for the way he'd behave. It wasn't as though this was a war you could feel too much about, anyway. He'd got away from his rotten and decaying comprehensive school, the mildewed house, concrete and brick walls – as a lot of the lads had. And the life in the Kate was all right. But this caper?

Of course, you couldn't let one country just barge in and snaffle bits of another country. But Trampas, for all his lack of education, felt something was askew here. He'd fight, for that was all he was good at. And it was a damn sight better than Ireland, where the Paddies at once aroused his utmost pity and his utmost hate. As time went on he had found his pity ousting the hatred. Poor sods. If you looked at Ireland and saw the beauty of the country, it made you wonder just why men and women were so damned stupid.

'Parley,' said Smyjo. He stood up again. 'If he doesn't

talk English – '

'You and me, Smyjo,' said Burnaby.

They started to walk out and the man in the overdressed suit raised his arms.

Andy called, 'Weapons.'

Annoyed, Burnaby handed his rifle back to Pugsy and Smyjo passed across his S.M.G. Why he wouldn't use a more modern weapon escaped Burnaby. It must be something to do with the Patchett. No doubt the silencer tickled Smyjo's imagination.

They walked on firmly, heads up, and ready to fling themselves flat in case the white flag this time was merely a ruse. You didn't stay alive too long in this game by trusting everyone implicitly.

The two parties halted some four or five metres apart and then the two British and the leading Argentinian approached to stand face to face.

A gust of wind whipped past, stingingly, while the Argentinian spoke liquidly and fluently, making gestures. Burnaby waited. He studied the fellow's face, all broken-veined and thin-lipped and pouchy-fleshed, disliking it on sight. From what he knew of Argentina's history – a sorry and blood-drenched affair – he knew that the rich stayed in power by shooting the poor or anyone who tried to oppose them. At election times, during almost all of the nineteenth century, they used to vote with rifles and artillery instead of ballot papers. They'd had a hard history and were a bloody lot because of that. If you could blame them, you could blame the bloody histories of England, too, as chronicled by Shakespeare.

Smyjo said, 'He's Captain Alvilas. Navy. That is probably not his real name. I guess he's the boss of one of those execution squads. He says we have no hope, we are surrounded, and we had best surrender.'

Burnaby, expecting just that, said, 'What else?'

'Nothing else.'

'You can tell him that as he claims to surround us he is clearly weaker at the place where we hit him. Tell him to go away quietly and we will do the same. You may add in your flowery Castilian that we don't want to kill more of his people. But we don't mind if we have to.'

The torrent of words that gushed from Captain Alvilas, even before Smyjo had finished, must, Burnaby decided, contain plenty of fruity obscenities. He turned away, and then swung back and glared at the naval captain.

Burnaby's face resembled that of a hanging judge sentencing a condemned man. Or, more accurately, that of an Anglo-Saxon warrior driving his sword into the guts of a Viking reiver.

'Ask him about Jock.'

When the swift Spanish gabble had finished, Smyjo said, 'He says Jock is badly wounded, but is safe.'

'Does he need hospitalization?'

The answer to that was in the affirmative. Burnaby then had to reconcile himself to the idea that they'd have to leave Jock. To move him in the difficult circumstances they faced would probably kill him.

The three men stood there for a moment in silence as the wind whistled mournfully past.

Testily, Burnaby said, 'Well? Is he going to clear off or not?'

'No,' said Smyjo. 'He insists we surrender.'

Burnaby turned around and started to walk off.

'You know what to tell him. And make it as insulting as you like. I can't stand the sight of the bastard.'

As they walked back, both Smyjo and Burnaby felt their backs to be as broad as barn doors. That the men of Strike Force had automatic weapons ready to open fire instantly was little comfort. The first two shots would be the only two that counted for Burnaby and Smyjo.

When they flopped back again Burnaby, for one, felt the ground under him as he'd feel the embrace of a solid concrete bunker. He breathed out hard.

'I've always been prepared to give a new person a chance. Always look on the decent side of a person. But that Argy gives me the creeps. If he'd shot us – '

'I'm surprised he didn't.' Smyjo held his S.M.G. after the manner of a man holding the cheque of a Pools win. 'They're an unstable bunch, so it's said – '

'True, though,' put in Pugsy.

'Not all. Their history is diabolical. Revolutions – well, you know it, I expect. They're not civilised in quite the way people ought to be civilised. At least, that is the impression they give.'

'That's the way they play football, too,' said Smart.

Hunkering down and staring out with an alert watchfulness, ready to leap instantly into action if the enemy attacked, Burnaby heard his own words ringing in his head. They rang mockingly. They rang ominously. What the hell had possessed him to say that? He'd said to Smyjo, 'As he claims to surround us he is clearly weaker at the place where we hit him.'

He licked his lips, and swallowed, and held onto his rifle.

It didn't need a military genius to know that. What his words might have done was to give this unpleasant slug of a Captain Alvilas some ideas. If he had, Burnaby would sure as hell say that it wasn't any wonder.

One thing was for sure, was for damned sure. He wasn't going to hang about here pinned down for ever whilst the Argies brought up thousands of blood-crazed commandos to blow them apart.

Pugsy was feeling like arguing with Smyjo.

'You said they weren't barbarians. Now you say – '

'I said that they're civilised differently from us. This bunch out here are probably more barbarian than the poor sods they've sent across to the islands.'

Andy cut in. 'We're in for some weather.'

The brightness had begun to fade from the day and the sky was becoming overcast. The wind was stinging unpleasantly. Visibility shrank.

Some poor devil the Argies had overlooked out there started to scream. They must have thought he was dead and ignored him. Now he had regained consciousness and was shrieking in agony.

The noise rasped at the men's nerves, but it had no power to disturb them unduly – no power as yet. You didn't get into Strike Force without facing the horrific possibilities inherent in war.

Trampas sat up.

The screams of agony built up. They would have frozen the marrow in the bones of anyone without the mental fortitude to face what had to be faced. Thankfully, after a moment or two of sustained, screeching agony, the voice fell away to bubbling groans that at last died.

The voice of Captain Alvilas called across the intervening distance. His words meant nothing until Smyjo translated. But before that Trampas, hand to his bandaged head, leaped up.

'That's Jock!'

And Smyjo cracked out, 'The bastard's torturing him until we surrender!'

CHAPTER NINE

'Still!' called Burnaby. He spoke with deliberate viciousness. For an instant, an instant only, Trampas wavered. Then soldierly discipline held him. He remained standing, hand to his bandaged head, glaring out into the shrouding mist.

'Sit down, Trampas.'

Trampas flopped down.

An Argie out there with a nightsight could pick up the greenish figure of the British soldier and send a 7.62 straight through his head.

Speaking calmly, Smyjo said, 'The decision's out of our hands, now. I'll need three men – two teams.'

'All right.' Burnaby spoke ungraciously. He knew he couldn't go himself. The Old Man was out of it, if only temporarily, and that left Burnaby to run the show. He did not wish Smyjo had been given the job – clearly the major had his reasons – but he did damn-well know that he'd dearly love to take the two teams out and strangle that bastard Alvilas and bring Jock back.

'I'm going.' Trampas's words slurred.

'Sawbones!'

'Here.'

'Well?'

Sawbones looked at Trampas.

'All right.' He half-turned away and spoke quietly to

Burnaby. 'He's perfectly fit and this will be the best medicine.'

Burnaby rounded on Smyjo.

'In your own time then, Smyjo.'

The swift professional arrangements for call signs and timings were rapidly finalised and then the mist swallowed up Smyjo, Trampas, W.O.II Smart and Brax.

The Whizz Kidd moved up to take cover position and Burnaby went off to the opposite side of the perimeter to check out Spider and Lawson.

The oppo system Strike Force used had been planned to take the best elements of that system and fuse them with the dictat of the major that any man should be able to work in a team with any other man. If your opposite number was killed, then, in Strike Force, you must not be allowed to feel alone and stranded. The natural feeling Trampas had for Jock was shared by them all.

The lurid, red rage in Trampas had to be contained, channelled, used. Old Jock was an uncouth heathen at times, but they'd been through it together and they worked well. Jock had stuck his chin out a few times for Trampas. Common origins in class, however far apart geographically they had been born, bound them in ways that Trampas was conscious of. As for Jock, he'd just grunt an almost-incomprehensible: 'Och, aye,' knowing how that infuriated the others. 'The officers is all right for some.' He meant he'd as lief kick an officer in the privates as salute him if he wasn't in Strike Force.

The weather could not be relied on. The cold was just cold and Trampas could cope with that. The equipment was first class. He prowled on following Smyjo, with Smartarse and Brax off to the left flank.

The going was not difficult. The ghostly figure of Smyjo looked like a wolf on the trail, lean and loping. Trampas checked all around as they forged on. They were up against crack troops, and not conscripts. Just how good the Argies were against other crack troops instead of terrorists and dissidents remained to be seen. Trampas had no doubts about his own and his comrades' abilities.

Part of those abilities had to be used with cold ferociousness to block out Jock's screams. What those bastards were doing to him Trampas did not know and did not wish to know. His fists gripped onto the armalite like talons. Whatever this Captain Alvilas and his gruesome bunch of thugs were up to, Trampas felt the inclination to inflict it on them with interest.

Alvilas shouted again.

Smyjo, up ahead, did not pause. Trampas, just able to sight that ghostly, wolf-like figure through the mist, padded on silently.

A man's voice shouted in return from the gully to the rear. The voice quivered. That would be Jorge, guessed Trampas, pressed into service by Tom Burnaby. The rapid Spanish babbled on for a space, and then Trampas saw Smyjo disappear.

Instantly, Trampas flattened.

He thought – he wasn't sure, he thought – he could hear three little sounds – plop, plop, plop.

An arm waved him on and he joined Smyjo.

A dead soldier lay sprawled. Smyjo peered ahead. In moments like this the men of Strike Force would touch hands and fingers and communicate by hand-sign language

There was no need for that now. Trampas waited the regulation time for Smyjo to move out and then followed, flanking, on guard, wary and ready to respond instantly.

They began to circle in towards the area where Jock was being tortured.

All the men of Strike Force could move swiftly and silently, stalk their quarry, kill quickly and efficiently. Of them all, Smyjo had a particularly chilling proficiency in this department. Big though he was, he somehow moved as though his feet did not touch the ground. The next Argie Trampas found had been killed silently in seconds and Smyjo was going smoothly on ahead.

Across on the other flank Smart and Brax were doing just the same. Jock's screams died out as the short exchange of shouts took place between Alvilas and Burnaby with Jorge as his translator. When they broke out again they sounded close, closer than Alvilas. Trampas frowned. Brax might save the bastard for Trampas. Smartarse most certainly would not.

The shrieking agony in Jock's voice keened into an intolerably high screech as though he had reached some ghastly barrier between his willpower and what was possible for a human being to withstand. The scream dwindled away, bubbling into a gargle that sounded to Trampas far too much like the last death rattle. He'd heard that sound before. He moved on with an urgency that came as much from controlled anger as from his reading of the situation – Smyjo would need him up close when they got there.

Noiselessly, wraithlike, they squirmed the last few metres on their bellies, weapons held just so, ready ...

What Jock had been through Trampas could only guess. He lay flat on his back, hands bound, his lower garments removed. Blood gushed everywhere about him. A man in camouflaged anorak was just standing up. At the end they must have used a slow castration on Jock, for the man standing up held the grisly dripping evidence in his fist.

Trampas jumped as though stung by a high-voltage shock. His armalite lay on the ground. He was on his toes, leaping forward, lunging. His left hand wrapped around the Argie's mouth, pressed hard against his head, and his right hand drew the commando knife across the throat. He leaned forward to take the body as it slumped and saw the dark spout of blood pour out and down the bastard's chest. Trampas eased the corpse to the ground and looked about.

Smyjo was a mere indistinct shape in the mist, about four yards off, a bulky, awkward figure. Trampas blinked. Then he saw that Smyjo had grasped another man, had his arm up his back and a hand across his mouth. Smyjo heaved and the man staggered backwards. He made some noise with his boots and Trampas dropped, reaching for his rifle.

Jock was dead.

Had he not been, Trampas had the sickly feeling he would have had a duty to put his oppo out of his misery, and he knew he wouldn't have been able to do that. He'd have carried him back and they'd have staunched the bleeding and bound him painfully up and when they got out of this and reached the hospital the medics would have put Jock back together again – all except the vital equipment that now lay on the ground, fallen from the hand of the dead man at Trampas's feet. That would have been no life for Jock.

Trampas looked once more on his comrade. There was no need to take paybook or identity discs. Smyjo came up. Without looking, Trampas held out his hand. Smyjo tapped, imperatively. Obediently, dazed, Trampas turned and followed. Jock …

That time in Aldershot with the barmaids, and the way they'd scampered off out of the fight, obeying the dictates of the unit which forbade bar-room brawls … Jock was a soldier, not a pub cowboy, all beer and mouth and no gutful of experience. Jock … The mist clung to Trampas's face, wetting his cheeks.

Jorge shouted again from back where Strike Force waited with no inkling of the tragedy.

Smartie and Brax heaved up, silently. Smyjo thrust his

prisoner across and Brax took him into a practised grip, hand across mouth, fist knuckling a trapped arm up cruelly. Trampas turned away and bent over.

Jock was no weight at all. Trampas held him cradled like a child, began to plod with the silent stalker's tread they all knew so well how to use, and followed on after his comrades.

Smyjo stayed out on the flank, to the rear, turning his head like the rear gun-turret of a Lancaster.

No one followed them, no one tried to stop them.

Trampas wanted to let rip a full clip into the bellies of these sadists, but he tramped on after the others, carrying Jock, feeling the blood greasily on his gloves.

For Tom Burnaby with Strike Force that period passed with agonising slowness. After Jorge, liberally prompted, shouted without receiving any further answers from Captain Alvilas, Burnaby reasoned that the silence meant a change in circumstances had taken place. He had to believe that change was a direct result of Smyjo's success. He had to ...

Mist clung damply to Burnaby's face and the day, if this miserable half-light could be called a day, struggled on. He had to believe that Smyjo had got in there swiftly and silently and rescued Jock. When Strike Force was re-united they'd move off and a bunch of Argies wouldn't stop them, no matter if they were some high-powered murder squad of professional killers.

He'd *had* to believe that Claire Havisham went through her strip act for obvious reasons – money. He'd tried to trace her at the London end but had met with no success, the refusal of information being in keeping with the club's attempts to protect the strippers. So he had had to go down to the Kent village and try from there.

She had not been at home when he called at the vicarage.

'She has a fine position in the City,' burbled the vicar, cheery, apple-cheeked, his white collar a choking glisten of glacier whiteness. Burnaby could see a similar collar around Claire's neck, his mind's eye summoning up the contours of her face and body, while her father rambled happily on about his daughter's prospects with the corporation and of her promotion to P.A. to the head of production. Burnaby found it difficult to breathe, and after the ritual cup of tea made his excuses and left.

He found a small clue to the puzzle in the vicar's information that Claire had never bothered her head over school; since her mother died she'd always been far more interested in extra-curricular activities. Burnaby got the impression that these had involved make-up, girls' magazines, modelling and mysterious giggle-filled conversations of interminable length on the family telephone. Claire had a younger sister who was quite different, called Anne, and the quarrels over the use of the telephone drove their father into the sanctuary of his study where he would prepare sermons on the evils of covetousness.

As a matter of course Burnaby wore civilian clothes on these occasions. He never volunteered the information that he was a soldier. He wondered, as he walked along the sunshine-filled country lanes, if Claire shared some of his feelings about her job – her home giving no clue to her profession. As a grammar school boy who'd had to fight tooth and nail to do anything he wanted, Burnaby well understood the theory of the underdog and the starkness of the displacement theory. His parents were upright, honest, hard-working, frightened of life and deadly dull. That was how Claire saw her father, too, with the added complication that as a churchman he could bring much bigger guns to bear in the guilt department.

The vicar had expressed surprise that Claire had secured

such a good position when one considered the lamentable state of her shorthand and typing. He was a firm believer in the value of a good Latin education, but allowed that creeping modernity must be involved, what with dictating machines and electronics and typewriters that wrote letters for you at the touch of a button.

Burnaby's interest in Claire Havisham intrigued him. Of course she was a splendid girl. She possessed a real beauty that could repel as much as attract if one was not prepared for its overpowering effect. The mysteriousness of the situation fascinated him just as much as any half-acknowledged desire to experience her brand of sex. But, then, the situation was not really mysterious. No doubt a psychologist would explain it simply enough. Burnaby just felt drawn to a further examination of the possibilities and if he and Claire hopped into bed together that would just be a natural consequence, a bonus, and, he devoutly trusted, an experience to cherish.

The thought of tracing his fingertips feather-light over her stomach and around her navel and drawing them gently through the shadows between her breasts gave him a delicious shuddery feeling of delight. Her skin, he felt sure, would be of a texture so soft and silky as to cry out for finger-painting. Feeling warm he went into The Royal Oak for a pint and an inspection of the bar lunches on offer.

The sun proved friendly enough for him to take his pint of Mackeson and his ploughman's out to the tiny garden where a scrubbed wooden table leaned against the roses. The sweet, rich scent of the flowers meant a great deal to him. He drank slowly, and pasted yellow butter on fluffy bread – an enormous chunk, half a cottage loaf – and ate Cheddar and thought about clergymen's collars, and pink nipples and slender legs, and generally came to the conclusion that he was a fully-blown, grade A1 silly idiot.

He'd just reached the point of considering the important

question of just how high black fish-net stockings should reach on perfectly shaped thighs so as to leave an appropriate amount of flesh exposed against which the suspender belt straps could be duly admired when Smyjo stomped up and threw a ragged bundle at his feet.

'Here's Alvilas, Tom.'

Nobody kicked the cringing man.

Trampas put Jock down. They covered him up and then they left Trampas alone for a short time. Whilst this went on the rest of Strike Force maintained constant vigilance.

Dolores crawled up. Quietly, Burnaby said, 'Smyjo. Tell Jorge to take Dolores back down the gully.'

When the two Argentinians had gone, Burnaby returned to his scrutiny of this famous Captain Alvilas.

'He's scared right through to his socks.' Smyjo caught his broad hand in the captain's collar and hauled his head round, the collar cutting into the man's neck. 'He'll start to stink soon.'

'Tell him we don't torture people. Ask him why he thinks we shouldn't just kill him right away, and have done.'

The quick babble of Spanish flowed and crescendoed, and after a savage order from Smyjo, softened to a whisper of pure fear.

'Umm,' said Smyjo. 'Now that's interesting. He says we shouldn't kill him because he has valuable information.'

'I'm not interested in the statistics of the dirty war – well, not right now.'

'He suggests it's not in the past – something to happen soon.'

There was very little Burnaby needed to consider in the immediate situation. 'As soon as the Old Man is fit to travel, we break out. The sub will be waiting by that time. We can't take Alvilas with us, so we either have to let him go or kill him.'

They glanced instinctively to the lumpen shape of Jock. Mist writhed and moved, glinting, and there was likely to be daylight again before night. Alvilas began to smell.

The Englishmen's looks were perfectly plain to the Argentinian, their meaning clear. He broke into a frenzied torrent of words, pleading, begging, kneeling up and thrusting his head forward in Smyjo's grip on his collar.

Burnaby caught fragments of words that might mean what they sounded like and probably didn't, that being the trap of foreign languages. He thought Alvilas said something about Exocet, but the pronunciation made it difficult to be sure.

Smyjo let out a whistling breath.

'Exocets,' he said. 'The bastards.'

'Well?'

'This turdhead says they're flying in a fresh supply of super-Exocets, secret deal, super-efficient missiles. They can wipe out the Task Force in one strike!'

CHAPTER TEN

The night pressed down, as dark and dank as the Duke of Hell's crotch. Burnaby scratched his cheek, reflecting on the vagaries of life and mainly on the diabolically tricky situation Strike Force now found itself in.

They'd buried Jock, properly, saying the right words, feelings pent up, and all the time keeping their heads down and the lookouts looking out.

Had Captain Alvilas curled up into a foetal ball, crooning and dribbling, no one would have been surprised. The man was insane with fear. After what he'd done to his prisoners in the Navy's Escuela Mecanica he must have expected the same hideous treatment. He was not a pregnant woman, so one of the Argie's favourite treatments couldn't be employed on him, but, as Brax said, he might be, given time, with the number of people willing to stuff him.

'You're sure he's told us all he knows?'

Smyjo brushed a finger across his upper lip. He looked, quite without meaning to, utterly superior.

'You can see the state the bastard's in. Whatever he knows, he's told us.'

Burnaby did not reply. He brooded on the huddled shape curled on the ground. He was a soldier and therefore in the business of killing people, but only certain people and only in the correct circumstances. He could not coldly kill Alvilas, despite the man's character, and the fact that the world would be better off without him. Burnaby did not believe he had the right credentials to pass that kind of judgement, let alone execute the sentence.

Spider came over from the hexi-stove with a mess tin.

'Does the stupid bugger want some chicken supreme?'

'Hardly,' said Smyjo.

'Not surprised,' said Spider, stirring the mess tin's contents morosely. 'Arctic rations ain't good news anywhere in the world, I suppose.'

Burnaby, who normally disliked turkey and chicken, agreed. The oatmeal biscuits in the rations provided by Strike Force's quartermaster genius went some way to keeping body and soul together. In addition, Burnaby, among most of them, liked to chew on an onion. Offended, Smyjo had once said that any enemy stupid enough not to smell a warning when Strike Force crept up on them deserved to be roasted.

'All we've gotta do is breathe on 'em,' Spider had amplified.

'Or use our other ends every third day,' commented Smart, referring to the general service rations' remarkable ability to induce constipation for three days followed by a liberation of pent-up forces frightening in their explosive lavishness. The men of Strike Force compiled a menu from many and varied sources, knowing they had to carry everything with them. And that their lives depended on enough intake was a powerful incentive to get the mix right.

Spider wandered off with his chicken supreme and no doubt he and Lawson would see that it was dutifully, if not pleasurably, consumed. Burnaby had to face the problem that had been presented to him, unwanted.

Because he had to fight this feeling of irritation, if not hostility, towards Smyjo, he reasoned aloud. 'We've taken out two targets so far, and if the other groups have done what they are supposed to do, then it's all hunky-dory.'

'Providing the Argies *haven't* any more coming in.'

'This turdhead Alvilas says they have. And super-Exocets, too, whatever they are. The Whizz Kid might know. At least, we ought to go across and suss it out.'

'The submarine is waiting, and the Old Man – '

'D'you fancy taking the major back?'

Smyjo did not react. He passed his forefinger across his upper lip, staring at Burnaby.

'No. Alvilas says these super-Exocets are being flown into the airfield at Castillos. If we march all out we might just reach there in time. But that's not our job, not in our orders.'

Here was another example of what the force's regard for Major Granville entailed. Smyjo was saying that they had to get the Old Man back to the submarine, and that was in their orders.

Speaking slowly and carefully, Burnaby said, 'I'll work out who goes back with the major and who goes with me to Castillos Field.'

The thought of slogging it all the way there and all the way back and hoping to find the sub still waiting did not fill him with any great enthusiasm – or optimism. What they might do at Castillos Field might brighten up the day a trifle. The Paras tabbed to and from and the Marines yomped, and other folk marched. It didn't matter what you called it; it was still lugging enormous great burdens over impossible trails and keeping up to schedule, and if you fell out – well, the men of Strike Force had been hand-picked by the major so that they wouldn't fall out. But it was going to be touch and go.

Burnaby told Pugsy to contact the submarine and inform them that this time the shore party would be detained. He made up his mind. Strike Force just had to go across to Castillos Field and prevent this fresh supply of Exocets from being used. If the major had to be carried back to the beach he'd spare two men. Just who he would send he would decide later.

Ollie Oliver, face black as sin, stormed in and dumped his machine gun. He began to spoon food into his mouth, grinding and chewing the soft stuff in a powerful expression of controlled rage. Thwackers, Cpl. Thwaite, looked across, did not follow, and settled back into position.

Burnaby watched the byplay, careful to betray no open interest.

'Bloody flower,' said Ollie Oliver around a mouthful. 'Wouldn't know a bass guitar from a piccolo. The narner.'

Thwaite looked balefully across, and then turned back to his scrutiny of his sector.

Strike Force was no bunch of angels. They were men of strong personality. Views were expressed with vehemence. Burnaby watched, not happy but content for the moment to let things roll. The major had his own particular way of handling problems. When the men blew their tops the froth had to blow away before situation normal could be resumed.

Andy came in for food. He said, 'There's absolutely nothing doing out there. I reckon with Alvilas gone missing they've all scarpered.'

'Could be.'

'Want me to go take a look?'

'Later on. When we break out.'

Smyjo said, 'Yes, break out. But which way?'

Burnaby did not answer.

Andy wanted to know if the submarine was ready yet.

Pugsy told him, 'She'll be there when we need her. But the Old Man might have to hang about a bit.'

'Oh?'

Oliver was grumbling away to himself. Burnaby heard him mutter, 'What does he know? Give me Generation X, or The Damned Stranglers. Billy Idle, f'instance – old Thwackers thinks the world ended after Status Quo.'

If that pair didn't sort themselves out damned quick they'd be in for what old Sergeant McArdle at Catterick would call a quantity of noxious effluvium from on high.

Burnaby again found himself mentally twitching. He had forced away his own dire premonitions about the way Strike Force had been selected, trained and led. Major Granville was one of the best, leather-tough, iron-hard, a man who had been through the mill and knew his business. His men would do anything he asked. But …

He turned his sour thoughts to his temptation to send off Smyjo with the Old Man back to the sub. That'd be one in the eye for the Woodentop, wouldn't it? But that idea was a non-starter. Smyjo was just too damned valuable to let go like that. Every member of Strike Force was valuable and irreplaceable; only in some departments one man was more equal than the others.

Pugsy came up and said in his harshest voice, 'You ought to get some shut-eye, Tom. I'm not carrying you.'

'All right, Pugsy.'

'You think I'm kidding, don't you? Try me and see.'

Finding a corner where he could curl up out of the wind, Burnaby flopped down.

For some reason he was dreaming of the time he'd managed to get Margie – or was it Marlene? – to come outside the disco. The night had been warm and muggy and the buttons on her blouse had slipped and slithered. She'd not made any attempt to help him. Her hair, all fair and haloed in a dim light from the front of the building, her face pale with dark blots of eyes and mouth, the feel of her under his hands – she'd just stood there, letting him.

He'd been entangled in the intricacies of getting his morse speed up to a respectable enough level to give him some hope of a continuing future in R.Sigs. When he'd got her bra off he found himself – and he'd never been able to recall just why – pressing her nipple in and out, sending morse. Di-di-di-dah-di, over and over. And, then, he sent, 'I love you'.

Her response shattered him. She reached down and grabbed him and pressed in and out, hard, and through his bemused state he realised she was sending morse too. She sent, 'You're a randy bugger,' and as he pulled her closer, she finished him off with, 'But I like it.'

She gripped his shoulder and shook him and he mumbled out, 'All right, I'm coming Margie – no, Marlene – ' and a girl's voice, accented, whispered in his ear, 'I must talk to you, Englishman.'

Instantly he was awake, aware, and glaring at Dolores in the eerie, green glow of a Betalight.

'Well? I was trying to sleep.'

'That man ... ' She took absolutely no notice of his acid comment, her dark face showing an emotion that Burnaby realised at once meant trouble.

His first shocked thought was that one of Strike Force had been trying to get his leg across, even in these unpropitious surroundings. It was not highly likely; but, then, too, it was not highly unlikely, either ...

'Who?'

'I am going to kill him, I think.'

'Who, for Christ's sake? And I'll strangle the stupid bugger first – '

She let go of his shoulder and rocked back on her heels at his violence. Her hair tumbled from the hood of her anorak and she pushed it back with an irritated gesture that told Burnaby she hadn't visited a hairdresser in too long a time.

She leaned forward again, and her breath fluttered warmly against his unshaven chin. 'Captain Alvilas. I think – '

'Oh, him! You had me going there for a minute. What about the noxious captain?'

'I am sure, I think, I am almost – certain – he is the man who took my brother and his wife away.'

'I see.' Burnaby could see, only too clearly. 'But you're not sure?'

'Almost.'

'Look, Dolores. Promise me you won't do – '

'I give no promises.'

In that uncertain glow she looked distraught, her eyes reflecting light in a way that gave her at once the look of mad frenzy and secret cunning. She wasn't really like that, Burnaby surmised, but by the time her emotions had been churned up by all that had happened she could do anything – and would, too, if she got half a chance.

'What's up?' Pugsy's whisper drifted in just loud enough to be caught.

'Squat, Pugsy.' Burnaby told him what Dolores had said. Pugsy tapped his teeth and said, 'Shoot the bugger and let's push on.'

'We don't know for sure, and right now he's a prisoner of war.'

'After Jock? People like him are animals.'

'That doesn't mean we have to be animals like them.'

Dolores spoke – in a way that showed the hurt she had suffered – without artifice, naturally. 'You may think you know answers, Englishmen. But who knows the happenings of the prisons? Torture is nothing. If a girl is with a baby – '

'Yes,' put in Pugsy. 'We have heard that one.'

'My brother Guillermo and Maria were to have a baby.' Dolores did not cry; had she done so it would have been less painful to listen to her. 'I would be the baby's aunt ... I have not seen them, heard of them ... '

Her English failed her then and she just sat rocking back and forth on her heels. Burnaby decided he could only act as he thought fit and could not allow private feuds to interfere with what had to be done.

Smyjo came up and before he could speak Burnaby told the intelligence officer to take Dolores off and find Jorge and try to calm her down.

'And don't let her near Alvilas.'

'Check.'

'And see if you can confirm her story. She's upset, so – '

'So I'll handle it, Tom.'

Burnaby nodded curtly and turned away in relief as Andy shuffled over, soundlessly.

'Andy – you still want to take a look-see out there?'

'Surely. Although there's sweet fanny adams, if you ask me.'

'Mosey out when you feel it right, then. We'll be moving off soon, so double-check on the inward leg.'

The sergeant-major started to move off and Burnaby checked him with, 'And we'll be dumping the jimpy. If you can liberate anything more useful out there ... '

Andy made no comment on Burnaby's decision.

'I'll have the supermarkets checked.'

'Use your credit card.'

'My bank manager's got high blood pressure. Wouldn't want to give him a stroke.'

When Andy left Burnaby decided to take another crawl around the perimeter. He refused to make any judgements on the state of the Argies out there. They might have run off. He tended to doubt that.

He was about to work his way cautiously to where Ollie Oliver crouched and tell him that his G.P.M.G. would be dumped on the next tab when Sawbones appeared.

About to make a testy remark about people jumping up like Jack-in-the-Boxes all over the place, he listened in shock to what Sawbones said.

'Tom. The major wants you, on the double.'

CHAPTER ELEVEN

Major Dan Granville – alert, fit, strapped-up, bursting with energy – got Strike Force moving quickly when Andy reported no sign of Argies. The men moved with caution and yet with certainty, bowed by the multiplicity of things weighing them down. Jaguar packs, bulging sacks of indeterminate origin, pouches, wallets, canvas flaps of ammo, cases for this and that, each man was a perambulating Woolworths.

Granville regarded Ollie with amazement.

'Leave the jimpy? Are you bereft of all senses, Ollie?'

'Tom said – '

'You, Ollie, are our artillery. Never forget that.'

'Check.'

Granville was bouncing with energy. He was polite to Burnaby, going so far as to thank him for carrying on after the major had been wounded. But things were Back To Normal now. The capital letters rang loudly in his words. Granville glowed. He was casually polite to Dolores, understanding to Jorge. Granville expanded. He showed Alvilas an indifferent contempt that, at the very least, was genuine. All in all, the major, the Dirty Old Man, was firmly back in the saddle.

Strike Force, humped under monstrous burdens, tabbed along after the major. Andy carried two rifles. The second he'd brought in from his brief recce as requested and now was reluctant to dump it. The Argies used the thirty round magazine instead of the twenty round box as supplied with the British S.L.R., and Andy considered this a not unreasonable artifact to acquire and use. Like many of the lads, he'd taped up two of the mags upside down so he could slap the empty out, reverse, and stick the fresh one back, all in the twinkling of an eye in the midst of combat.

Burnaby said to him, 'Dump the damn thing, Andy. It's just extra weight now.'

'Far be it from me either to argue with an orffizer or to carry an ounce I don't have to, Tom. But – well, Pugsy contacted the sub and she's waiting as per schedule now. So ... '

'All right. It's your back and legs.'

And, of course, here was the rankling, unreasonable reason for Tom Burnaby's hopeless feelings of being caught in a mill race and swept away. Mission accomplished, the major had announced. Strike two Exocets plus two Super Etendards. So, home, lads. Back to the sub. He had dismissed out of hand the tale of the super-Exocets as related by Captain Alvilas.

'All moonshine, dear boy. Suck us in, get us to tab inland for miles and then jump us when we get there and find nothing. A trap. Open and shut.'

'But – '

'Act your age, Tom!'

'Alvilas is so consumed by terror he's incapable of inventing anything like that, of telling anything but the truth.'

'Cunning little buggers, people like him. They trap people as a way of life. I'm sorry about the girl's brother and sister-in-law. But that's all a part of it. Dirty stuff. I expect the human rights people will want to ask this Alvilas thing a few questions.'

The going was difficult, and the men kept on in a way

that spoke eloquently of training that carried simple muscles and plain flesh and blood beyond all the thresholds of rationality. They marched on willpower.

Unburdened, the three Argentinians were just able to keep up.

There was no sign of pursuit, but Burnaby, for one, did not think the Argies would remain inactive for long. They did not relish enemies walking about in their land any more than any other folk would.

For a time Dolores walked alongside Burnaby. She panted and held her head up, and breathed hard, but she kept on going. She even managed to gasp out a few words.

'Why do you not let me see this Alvilas?'

'All in good time, all in good time.'

'But – '

'Save your breath.'

She strode along in silence, breathing hard, and then she said, 'My friends' home must be close now. Perhaps I will go there with Jorge.'

'Why not.'

Up ahead the Old Man led off with virile energy and if he felt any twinges of pain from his wound he did not let them hinder him.

Brax said to his oppo, 'Sawbones must have stuffed the Old Man so full of pills he rattles.'

'Naw,' corrected Smart. 'He's got so many pills inside him there's no room for 'em to rattle.'

After that it was a question of keeping the lungs open, the tongue still and the legs walking. No one wasted breath. But, having forced unwilling bodies along before in enormously extended route-marches – route-runs, more like – the men were able to relapse into a kind of semi-conscious thinking.

Provided the eyes kept scanning the surrounding landscape for potential danger, the brain could be allowed to dwell on happier times. In the midst of misery you returned mentally to happier times. This was a trick used by the Jerries on the Russian Front. Extremes of cold and privation could be endured if the brain spent most of its time imagining warmth and feasts and pretty girls. This was a technique that had proved itself.

Whilst Ollie Oliver of the spiked orange hair pulsated away to Siouxsie and the Banshees, and Thwackers tinkered with the oily insides of an MG Magnette, Pugsy came in from a romping run with Sasha, all paws and tongue and lolloping affection, to a glorious romp with Jonie, to whom much the same descriptions applied. It was just as well she got along so splendidly with Sasha, for his Alsatian took to friends and did not take to some folk. Pugsy always allowed that Sasha knew best, and steered his own course accordingly. As for Jonie, when they were married he did not think he'd allow the Napoleon and Josephine syndrome to apply. Nothing was coming between him and what Jonie had, not even a remarkable, affectionate idiot Alsatian called Sasha.

Brax and Smartie humped along together, solid, reliable, enormous men, hairy and ruffianly and completely unrecognisable to anyone of their parent units.

Each man's thoughts turned to those secret areas which sustained him, and each man was ready instantly to hurl himself into cover and return fire with flame and steel – as the saying had it. As the Old Man used to say, 'You won't catch my lads with their trousers down, not even in the lavatory.'

When they halted for a brief, routine breather Burnaby made another effort. He rounded up Smyjo and went along to the crevice in the boulders where the Old Man sat propped up, beaming, in great spirits, on top of the world.

'Smyjo,' Burnaby started. 'You heard what Alvilas said,

at first hand. The major just has to be made to believe it – '

'Hold on, Tom.' Smyjo's face expressed nothing of what he might be thinking. 'I believe the Old Man to be right. He always is. We should have spotted it ourselves.'

'But – '

'Look, Tom. This Alvilas fellow is used to handling suspects, terrorists, and trapping them. He put on that scared act. I must admit I thought it a little overdone at the time.'

Burnaby fumed, but he kept his rage pent up and did not burst out with the perfectly natural, 'Oh, come *on*!'

They reached the major and stood, a little awkwardly, before him.

'Yes, Tom?'

'Major. I honestly believe what Alvilas says. We can't just go on back to the sub and leave this new supply of Exocets to be flown in – '

'Fairy stories!'

'I don't think so.'

'Smyjo?' Granville looked casually up. 'You're the intelligence officer. You talk the language. What's your appreciation?'

'I agree with you, Major.'

What the hell could he say? How could he make them share his own horrible conviction? Alvilas *was* speaking the truth, Burnaby was absolutely certain of that.

'Alvilas says the plane with the super-Exocets is due to fly in tomorrow or the day after. If we start now we can get there in time – '

'We only have food for two more days, Tom.'

'So we march hungry! Or we snaffle a sheep. If we tamely run off now and those Exocets sink the Task Force – '

'That won't happen.' The major sounded confident and forceful, supremely in command.

Faintly, rising and falling, the chopping beat of a helicopter reached them from the north.

'We're due company.' The major brisked up even more, if that were possible with all the pills stuffed into him.

Strike Force disappeared. They vanished, as it were, into the very ground. Ponchos covered them, they lay in slits and holes, weapons ready, and any chopper pilot who picked them out would have to have X-ray eyes.

The noise of the helicopter faded, roared out one more time and then ceased. The only sound was the wind soughing over the barren land.

Presently the major called softly, 'Tom. A little recce seems in order.'

'Very good.'

'Got to know what the beggars are up to. You'd better go yourself. Take Pugsy.'

'I'd rather like to keep Pugsy on the set, Major – '

'No. Give him a run. Do him good.'

You didn't argue with Major Granville when he gave an order like that. No one wore rank badges, of course, and they used nicknames as part of their normal lives, and they all mucked in. But no one forgot there was a chain of command, with Major Granville at the top of the heap.

Burnaby crawled across to the Scimitar and spoke quietly to Pugsy.

'The major wants us to take a look see. It's probably friends of Alvilas come to find out what happened to him.'

Pugsy took off the headset and Spider eased over.

'And treat that wireless like a new-born baby!'

'Like a luscious topless disco dancer,' said Spider. 'Your baby's in good hands, Pugsy.'

'You'd give anybody kittens, you would.'

Burnaby did not smile at his comrades' antics. They were trained and knew what they were doing and were aware of the value of the equipment they used. But they were not in awe either of equipment or their own reputations. The British Army kept going on humour, very often all they did have between them and the terminal horrors. Burnaby and Pugsy, stripped of all inessential gear, gripping their rifles, moved out.

The weather remained foul. In these conditions you had to put the state of your body out of your mind, firmly confine it to an area marked, 'Out of Bounds. Investigate later.' You marched all night and lay up during the day, invisible, dug in under camouflage, and – like now – you recced aggressively if anything untoward occurred.

They backtracked for a bit and then struck off at an angle to the line of march. Cautiously, they probed forward.

Alert for the first sounds of opposition, Burnaby and Pugsy made a formidable team. Yet there were only two of them, and for all they knew a whole battalion of Argies might be lying in wait for them.

Burnaby wanted this thing over with and himself and Pugsy safely back with Strike Force with the first rising of the mists.

Distantly, like a pack of berserk Baskerville hounds, the sound of dogs reached them. They halted, silent, listening. The hounds howled mournfully, as though desolate at the sins of the world and then, sharply, suddenly, they broke into shrill yelps and staccato barking.

'They've picked up our trail,' said Pugsy. 'My Sasha was always too sloppy and friendly to – '

'They'll follow right into the lads,' interrupted Burnaby.

He felt hot and cold at once, gripped by the sudden realisation that if those dratted dogs sniffed them out they'd all be done for.

'Once they get onto the scent,' confirmed Pugsy, 'they'll follow right on. Too right.'

'So – '

'It goes against the grain, though.'

'Yes.'

They kept low and moved out, quartering back to the trail Strike Force had followed earlier. Burnaby could feel the blood forcing itself through his arteries and veins, a solemn thudding pulse that did nothing to reassure him. His throat was dry. He could do with a wet around now. The mist began to coil, evilly, like the fumes from the cauldrons of the three witches in Macbeth.

Moving with exquisite, silent care they came down to a gully almost walled by stones, with a little scrub bent and contorted by the wind. There'd be a fine fancy Latin name for this scrubby vegetation; Burnaby couldn't care less. Pugsy moved on ahead, a dim figure, bulky and sure, moving soundlessly.

The ululation of the dogs reached them like the wailing of banshees, caught by the wind, swelling and dying. It was almost impossible to judge how far away the bloodhounds were.

Although, Pugsy reflected as he edged along the gully, they'd more likely be Germans, or Alsatians, perhaps. That time Sasha got herself entangled with that sloppy Dalmatian, why, it had been like a sausage and egg in a too-hot frying pan. That had been in the park just about Daffodil time, and Jonie had laughed and laughed, not worrying that the wind flicked her green skirt up, that the park keeper was gawping, and the grey-haired old lady trying to rescue her stupid Dalmatian was thrashing away with her stick.

'Steady on, missus,' and Pugsy jumped forward, incensed. 'Sasha's too friendly to hurt a fly. Your sausage machine is all right.'

'Dogs like that oughtn't to be allowed – '

He'd grabbed Sasha, hugging her, and hauled her off, and the Dalmatian looked up with those black-marble eyes and Pugsy could swear he'd been enjoying himself, too.

Dogs liked to romp just as much as humans.

Sasha was falling all over him, licking at him, big and lumpy enough to knock him over if he didn't watch out. Jonie told the grey-haired old lady a home truth that made her gasp, and the Parkie strutted up when it was safely all over, looking important.

'People are frightened of big dogs like that,' he said. 'You oughta keep him on a lead.'

'She's a she, and she's on a lead. It was the sausage machine who got off the lead.'

The Parkie sniffed and Sasha gave a shrill and quite unladylike yelp, and Pugsy saw down the stony gully the indistinct figure of a man and, leaping out ahead of him, the shapes of dogs.

He saw the lead dog quite clearly. She looked just like Sasha. He lifted his rifle.

The dogs stopped howling. They raced in for the kill.

Just like Sasha, even to the markings –

'Shoot, Pugsy, shoot!'

Burnaby, masked by his comrade's bulky body, saw the dog bunch, saw it leap. Pugsy went down. For a single horrific instant Burnaby saw the ugly glitter of yellow fangs. Then the dog tore out Pugsy's throat.

Burnaby lifted his rifle. He shot three times, three times at that first bastard dog that had killed Pugsy. He swivelled and triggered three more at the second dog, and three more at the third.

Someone down the gully shot back, and the bullet whined off rock. Burnaby didn't care about the stupid human with a rifle shooting at him. He lined up on the last dog and felt rock chips splatter him as a round splashed against the boulder at his left. He missed his shot and the dog leaped and he had to jump aside, moving like a marionette.

The Bullpup Personal Weapon didn't have much of a

butt; Burnaby used what butt it did have to smash down on the dog's skull. The harsh metal broke through the bone. He smashed again, and again, and again.

He could hear rifle fire.

He looked up madly, glaring, wild with fury.

Two men appeared, both wearing the parka-type anoraks with hoods affected by the Argies. He shot them both, and then gave another savage smash at the bleeding broken head of the dog.

He was panting.

He walked over to where Pugsy lay. Sergeant Albert Battersby, Royal Corps of Signals, lay as though asleep. His body was fully regimental, with equipment and clothing in perfect order. His face looked surprised, and was unmarked.

His throat looked like a butcher's slab.

The blood-smell tasted raw, offensive in his nostrils. He shivered. He didn't know what to think. Pugsy was dead, and that was all there was to it. Dead. Just in a twinkling. The feral leap, the fur flying through the air, the slashing, rasping wrench of teeth, and skin, flesh, blood, ripped and shredded and torn away. Bloody mess everywhere. And Pugsy was dead.

Burnaby kicked the dog's body away, and then kicked it again. He had to get hold of himself. He was supposed to be a cool, calm professional fighting man. Supposed to be …

A tiny fraction of that cool professionalism made itself felt in an incongruous way through the clamour of horror and grief. The small bullets had done their job. Three had been just about enough. He hadn't even bothered to calculate if one would have done. He'd look forward to testing that out. He straightened up, listening intently.

If the chopper had brought in a search party, then he must have blunted the sharp end right here. There would be more of them, but he could hear no more dogs.

He's used four times three shots, and then two. So he had six left in the mag. As he walked cat-footed down the valley-like depression he took out the mag and slipped in a full clip. He reached the two Argies and looked down. One's head was a bloody mess, half of the back blown away. The other was still alive with a bullet lodged somewhere in him, coughing blood in a weak dribble down an unshaven chin.

Burnaby turned him over, made him as comfortable as he could, put his dead comrade's anorak over him and then shoved his rifle butt uppermost into a cleft in the rock.

'If your mates find you, you'll be all right. If they don't, then you'll be like Pugsy.'

The man moaned. Burnaby looked about, saw nothing, listened, heard nothing out of the ordinary, and turned away.

'If your evil junta hadn't tried to steal something that wasn't theirs, you wouldn't be here and likely to die, and Pugsy wouldn't be dead. If you expect me to feel sorry for you, don't bother. Or any of your lot.'

As he walked back up the gully he was well aware of his own reactions. He was educated enough to know that this was what happened in wars. You could call the process by any number of fancy names. The sensibilities became blunted. It was not a simple matter of vowing revenge for the death of a comrade. In wars men died, anybody knew that. Only the reality was always different from the expectation. Even Jock's death, for all the gruesomeness of his end, hadn't affected Burnaby quite like this. The reasons were easy enough to find.

He went back, picked up Pugsy, not caring that the blood smeared over him, draped him over his shoulder, took his rifle, and started back for Strike Force.

If any Argies had met him, and even had he been killed,

they would have suffered badly at his hands. He'd have shot every last bastard of them, and still taken care of what was left of Pugsy.

Despite all his natural humanity, despite being a decent sort of man, he couldn't help those feelings. He just hoped he would get over them, in time. If he wasn't killed dead before that ...

CHAPTER TWELVE

Each member of Strike Force took Pugsy's death, as they had Jock's, in his own individual and private way.

Some of them – Spider and Lawless for sure – would feel that blind murderous rage and desire for revenge that troubled Burnaby. Smyjo's reactions, which normally baffled Burnaby, remained as impenetrable as ever. Andy looked withdrawn, grim in his trained and unemotional way. But he suffered, Burnaby knew that. Brax and Smart would not spare an Argie Special Commando man in the future. Conscripts – well, they might or might not be brushed aside like levies chained and stapled to the ground. But Strike Force was up against professionals like themselves.

Burying Pugsy with due propriety was complicated by the anti-surveillance routine in force. They could not stand with bowed heads around the graveside. But they buried Pugsy properly, anyway, and crouched low as the major read the appropriate passages. Dolores and Jorge, a little way back, also paid their respects to the dead man. Argentinian earth scattered down, rock chippings and dirt, and Pugsy was laid to rest.

Burnaby ate some gunk slopped out by Spider, not knowing or caring what it was, and then he got his head down. The major's firm decision to regard the mission as complete depressed Burnaby. He could not alter that. He tried to get some sack time in, and dozed, and was aware of the bleak landscape and also of black fish-net stockings and white thighs, and the way that white clerical collar with its cusp of lipstick tantalised him as it embraced Claire's throat.

Their next meeting had deepened the mystery.

The gentleman of foreign extraction at the strip club categorically refused to impart any information on the girls. He was polite.

'But – ' said Burnaby.

'I must ask you to leave, sir. All the girls are respectable ladies.'

'I don't doubt it. But, you see, I – '

He'd put his hand in his pocket, quite automatically, thinking nothing of it, or, had he done so, only to keep the clenched fist out of sight.

'Please do not attempt to bribe me, sir. I am not running a bordello, or even an escort agency here. Please do not make a scene.' As those liquid eyes indicated the shadowy presence of a large and craggy gent in an ill-fitting suit standing passively in the archway, Burnaby conceded a temporary set-back and saw that a planning withdrawal was the only option.

Later, he reasoned that the punctilious speech and the ultra-refined moral tone indicated that the man must have taken Burnaby for the police. He might not know all the men on the vice squad. He had a living to make and would take no chances. Introductions had to be impeccable before he would reveal his hand.

So, one weekend when he was off duty, Burnaby again went down to Kent, ostensibly to visit his aunt. She was pleased to see him, making some comment quite without artifice, that he'd taken to coming down to visit a lot lately, and that was very nice. Burnaby smiled and agreed, and did the washing up and then went off to the local.

A farmer called Bill Appleby, whom he knew slightly, engaged him in conversation. Appleby rented an acreage that would never make him a millionaire – even with the crazy E.E.C. regulations in force – but was enough to ensure he'd not starve. He was a tall fellow, a little sallow, with a slight stoop and the way farmers have of speaking as though they live on the edge of disaster.

They drank a couple of pints, talking of nothing in particular, and then the group Appleby was with insisted on going along to the Duck and Drake where they said real ale was real ale.

Burnaby went along, driven by Appleby in his Landrover. He didn't care much for real ale, despite its undoubted superiority over gaseous bottled stuff. He liked Mackeson. But Burnaby, at a loose end, was quite content to soldier on and see the evening out in company he found undemanding and friendly. He was not a foreigner to these folk in quite the same way that he would have been if, say, he'd moved down from London and lived there for twenty years.

The Duck and Drake, set at a crossroads surrounded by fields and not much else, was all low beams and angled roofs and ingle nooks and horse brasses that were the genuine article and not Brummagem circa nineteen fifty. A permeating, homey smell of honey and roses clung to the building, which had probably seen Cromwell's Ironsides drinking there one day and Charlie's Cavaliers the next.

A good deal of laughter filled the bar, and men and women settled down to the serious weekend pursuits of drinking and what followed. The most noise erupted from a group of youngish men dressed in hacking jackets, and expensive slacks, and fifty-guinea appendages to the well-dressed gent in the country. Their shoes were hand-made. They talked loudly. Their cars were parked outside, Lotus, Porsche, that kind of quality. Their faces were mostly red, beefy, well-fleshed, and their gestures were expansive. Appleby and his friends merely nodded and sat in a corner where Burnaby cradled his pint and watched, talking when spoken to.

Claire Havisham walked in.

The man with her had slicked, dark hair, a thin, black moustache, and wore jeans and a leather coat. They ordered gins and tonic and sat down. Burnaby suddenly felt aware of the heat of the room.

What followed was inevitable and tawdry and extremely unpleasant. Trying to sleep in his sack on the rocks of the inhospitable Argentine mainland, Burnaby turned restlessly. The way people reacted, the way they seemed to be forced to behave by their own natures, and by fate, and by sheer stupidity, never ceased to amaze him. Was everyone a mere puppet?

The group of young, high-powered local gentry began to laugh. They were all looking at Claire and her companion. What they said in those loud, hectoring voices brought the other conversations in the pub to silence.

'Of course it is! No mistaking that, is there?'

'You're sure, Mark?'

'Absolutely! When you've seen what she's got, all hanging out, I tell you, sport, you're not going to forget it.'

Burnaby sat quietly.

One of the hacking jackets and hand-made shoes and expensive slacks hoisted itself to its feet and weaved across to Claire's table. Its companions yodelled as they must have done coursing, and followed in a clamouring group.

'Play the damned music, Simon!'

The one called Mark leaned over, leering.

'We'll pay, so go through your act. It's all clean fun!'

'Get 'em off!' someone yelled from the back.

They fell about laughing.

Claire's companion stood up. He looked green,

uncertain, and he clutched the back of his chair.

Claire said, 'It's all right, Paul.' She looked up, admirably firm. She spoke quietly. 'Go and sit down, Mark. You're being tiresome.'

'Tiresome! Why, you little whore – I know who you are! You're old Havisham's daughter, and you strip – '

'Sit down, Mark!'

Paul put a hand to his lips under that strip of moustache. He looked unhappy. 'What are you talking about?'

'Shut up, you silly little man. You her pimp?'

Paul looked shattered. 'I don't know what you're talking about. But you can't insult – '

Mark put a broad hand in Paul's face and pushed. Leather jacket collapsed back into the chair.

'Shut up!'

The flush of blood staining along Claire's cheekbones gave her the look of a woman about to explode in a fury. She drew in a sharp breath.

'I think you are insufferable, Mark. You seem to have mistaken me for someone else – '

'Oh, no. No, that won't wash. I've seen you starkers, strutting up there on the stage. I've seen what you've got, my girl, and we're going to see it again, right now!'

A transistor radio was produced and the one called Simon rotated the knobs until he chanced on a station hammering out a suitable heavy beat. He pushed the radio forward, and Mark put a hand on Claire's shoulder.

'Up on the bar, girl, and start. We'll pay!'

Paul made a last effort, struggling to rise, and was quickly and efficiently pinned down by a couple of Mark's companions. They learned that kind of skill playing rugby, and afterwards, when they wrecked hotels.

Appleby put a farmer's hand on Burnaby's arm. 'I don't like it, Tom. But it's none of our business.'

'Maybe I should make it my business.'

'They're the local nobs. If you cross them – '

'Then it's my look out.'

'Tom – '

But Burnaby stood up, carefully putting his glass down. Strike Force and its parent unit most strictly forbade bar punch-ups. The men of S.S.F. did not go in for pub brawls. They were soldiers, not bar-flies. But this situation was different from an argument with the green berets or the crap hats, or, if it turned out that way, with the Maroon Machine itself. He walked forward slowly.

Claire did not see him as he advanced.

Burnaby was not foolish enough to put a hand on Mark. He halted and wet his lips. 'I do not think the lady wishes to – '

Mark, still gripping Claire's shoulder, swung about. His face was beet-red. His eyes looked feverish. 'Lady? She's just a stripper, a whore. This is nothing to do with you. Just push off – '

Claire saw Burnaby. She looked surprised. Not pleased, not relieved, not alarmed. Just surprised.

'Just let the lady go and sit down.' Burnaby spoke calmly. 'This has gone far enough.'

'I don't know who you are, chum – but I'm in a good mood.' Mark did not release Claire's shoulder. His face had that over-ripe, pumped-up look of glassy feverishness associated with moments of heightened awareness, of gallons of extra adrenalin flushing through the system, of consciousness of power and enjoyment. 'This girl may be a vicar's daughter down here. Up in town she's a stripper. I thought it was her when I saw her. My God! She's a beauty, and I think the fellows would like to see what she's got. So, chum, go away and sit down.'

Even in his over-ripe condition, Mark must have sensed that this stranger was not in the same league as Paul.

Someone at the back yelled, 'Clear off, you idiot! Mark's

a karate expert – ' The rest, concerning the colour of his belt, was lost in the jeers and catcalls of his cronies.

Trying to carry this thing off and thoroughly detesting the whole sordid scene, Burnaby spoke in his open, affable way, as though talking to a recruit hesitant about the Tarzan Walk. 'You must be mistaken. Miss Havisham – '

Mark shouted. 'Simon, Mac, trundle this little pest away, will you?'

Eager to oblige, his grinning friends jumped forward, openly enjoying what was to come.

Old Sawbones had gone through the various pressure points, which as a doctor he used to cure people and which, as he pointed out with due sorrow, the men of Strike Force would use to incapacitate people. Keninja as a system combined much of other martial arts and much of Western philosophy and physical aggression, and the resultant mix was potent indeed. Burnaby did not rate himself as A1 in Keninja. He left that level of superb expertise to people like Smyjo. But he knew what he knew.

He put a thumb into the appropriate point just off Simon's left breast and didn't bother to watch him fall down, so fast was the action. He clipped Mac just under the jawbone, alongside his under-ear, and Mac, too, fell down.

'Just let the lady go,' he said. 'And we'll call it a day.'

'Oh no we won't, you bastard!'

And Mark went for him like a berserker.

Whatever colour his karate belt may have been, it would have been drenched blood red in other circumstances as Mark bored in, hands weaving. Keninja saw him off in a nice peaceable way, slumbering with his head under a table and a pint of best bitter, inadvertently knocked off, dripping onto his flushed face.

'Tom!'

'None of my business, Claire. But, perhaps you and Paul had better – '

'Yes. Thank you.' She stood up, her face drained. Burnaby wondered if that was a result of having her secret trumpeted in a taproom, of the incident itself, or merely of the violence that had erupted and finished almost before it began. Paul tottered to his feet.

Burnaby glanced back. Only an idiot left his rear unrecced. The gang of upper-class-twits clustered, hovering, not sure what to do. Appleby caught Burnaby's eye and gave a slight nod of his head towards the front door. The meaning of his gesture was unmistakable.

He said, 'Do you mind if I tag along for a bit?'

Paul shrugged his leather coat straight. The arms looked as though they'd never had flesh and blood arms thrust through them.

'Glad to. Pigswill in here, that's God's truth.'

'Not all,' said Burnaby equably, and went with Claire and Paul out to his Capri.

He climbed in and leaned back on the seat at the rear and for a moment thought Pugsy was nudging him awake with a cup of tea.

'All right, Pugsy. I'm awake.'

'It's Spider, Tom. And there's no tea.'

He was awake instantly.

He cursed himself.

Pugsy would never again – forget it. Concentrate on the objective and get the hell out of this godforsaken spot.

'Right, Spider. What's the situation?'

'The sub's on line waiting. We just tab down to the beach and go home.'

Smyjo loomed up. 'That's right, Tom. We've done our job. It's all over bar the shouting.'

Burnaby thought but did not say, 'It may be all over. But I'm not done shouting.'

CHAPTER THIRTEEN

Moving against the rocks like a chameleon, Tom Burnaby wriggled up to Ollie and Thwackers in their pit on the perimeter.

'Nothing stirring. The chopper pulled out before Smart and Brax got to it.'

'Pity.'

Head low, Burnaby scanned the featureless terrain. Or, rather, the terrain. A billiard table was not featureless to a man trained in counter-surveillance techniques. He did not think it at all likely; but there *could* be a company or three of Argie Special Forces out there right now. He checked the quadrants and knew he'd see nothing that Ollie and Thwackers hadn't already seen and noted. He wriggled back, low and easy.

'We'll be moving out soon.'

'Can't be too soon.'

'And you still have your jimpy, Ollie.'

'Major's orders, Tom.'

'Yes. Andy won't chuck that damn S.L.R. he found away. Bothers me.'

Thwackers showed with a flash of teeth.

'Trophy of war.' He guffawed, but quietly.

'Give me a picklehaube every time,' said Burnaby, and wormed his way back and down and went off to check the other side, where Lawless remained invisible until you fell over him.

'Nothing, Tom.'

'We're moving out soon. What are your thoughts on Pugsy's wireless?'

Lawless did not reply at once, giving the question its due share of consideration. Finally, he rolled his gum to the other side of his mouth and said, 'If we're tabbing down to the sub, reckon Spider and me can cope.'

'All right. But I want you and Spider at the sub, with or without the wireless. If it becomes too much, dump it. It's only money.'

Then Lawless said, 'Pity about them super-Exocets.'

For a treacherous moment, Burnaby felt like saying something to the effect that he was glad someone else shared his opinion, but that would mean calling into question the Old Man's edict. That would never do for Strike Force as run by Major Dan Granville.

'Yes,' he said at last, trying to make the word neutral.

On the third side of the triangle Trampas held himself in a way that looked suspicious to Burnaby. In his casual, easy, open way, Burnaby checked the report and then said, 'Feeling okay, Trampas?'

'Sure.'

Burnaby gave Trampas a good, hard stare. He let Trampas feel Burnaby looking at him. Trampas held that stare for a moment, and then he looked away, and licked his lips.

'Truth is, Tom – don't feel on the top line.'

'Right.'

'You won't tell the major ... ?'

'No need. We're moving out. If you have to L.I.B. something, do it.'

'I was figuring on giving Spider and Lawless a hand with the wireless.'

Trampas didn't mention Pugsy.

'They'll cope. I want you back at that sub in one piece. Capisch?'

'Capisch.'

Moving back to the gully, Burnaby reflected that if Trampas did dump any gear, the claim that it was Lost In Battle – L.I.B. – would be perfectly correct. The saying that men were more important than equipment might be trite, banal, overdone; but it remained true, and nowhere more true than with the personnel of Strike Force. Mind you, they'd run through a few scenarios in which the delivery of vital equipment over-rode even the preservation of men's lives. If that had to be done, Strike Force would do it, and not count the cost. Here, right now, it did not apply.

Determined to have a go at Andy and force him to drop that stupid rifle he'd found, Burnaby got back to the gully in time to see Dolores fling herself on Captain Alvilas.

The experiences through which she had gone, the grief and terror, the remorseless erosion of everything that was precious to her, gave her muscles and blood and bones an elemental fury. It was as though she leaped in just revenge for all of miserable Argentina. Her nails, broken and dirty though they were, slashed down Alvilas' face, drawing blood. He staggered back, arm upraised, yelling in surprise. She ravaged him like a lioness, kicking, biting, scratching. And she panted out venomous words as she fought, hair swirling, face inflamed, engorged on fear-fuelled anger and revenge.

Smyjo hauled himself up from the ground where the completely unexpected attack by the girl had tripped him. She was a wild fury. A wildcat would have been a tame tabby in comparison.

He jumped forward, calling to her in Spanish. He saw at once that no words would stop her. Alvilas, blood glistening over his face, tried to punch the girl and she kicked him in the crotch and he doubled up, screaming.

She bashed at his head as he went down.

'Leave off, leave off! Stop it! You'll kill him!'

'I will! I will!'

Alvilas had a spark, no matter what he was. He had given himself up for lost when the English captured him. But – this *girl*! This *woman*! Despite the pain coursing through his body he groped for her, determined to smash her down for good and all.

With that resurgence of energy in the man who had kidnapped her brother and sister-in-law, who had done unthinkable things to them, Dolores became completely uncontrollable.

Smyjo staggered and his Sterling slithered forward on its sling. He tried to grab Dolores and she twisted like a salmon out of his hands. Smyjo's boot turned on a loose rock.

With a shriek of pure triumph, Dolores snatched the Sterling. She knew how to use an S.M.G.

She lifted the snub weapon, turned the muzzle on Alvilas. He saw. He yelled and with a convulsive leap tried to jump for cover among the rocks of the gully. Dolores pressed the trigger.

The rounds racketted out. Some caught Alvilas as he sprawled among dust and rock chips, others sprayed across Major Dan Granville as he hurried up.

Then Smyjo had girl and S.M.G. in his grip. He simply twisted the weapon away and pushed her down. He looked in appalled horror as the Major slumped forward.

Men ran in, shattered, Tom Burnaby leading the rush, far too late, separated from tragedy by time and distance and treacherous rocks.

Neither man was dead.

In the aftermath of that ugly scene, Burnaby said something he instantly regretted. 'You fool, Smyjo!'

'Later.' Smyjo just didn't turn around. He bent to the

major and with Sawbones – immediately there – set about making the Old Man comfortable and tending to his wounds. Three bullets had hit Granville, two of which would have been merely inconveniencing. The third was lodged in his chest and Sawbones shook his head as he examined the wound.

'Well?'

Sawbones looked up. His face was drawn.

'The Old Man's tough. But this ... I can see about these two. The one in his chest – we must carry him to the sub. And damned quick. We can't hang about.'

'Right.'

If the doctor said the major could be moved then he knew what he was talking about. They'd carry the Old Man all the way to the sub and there the surgical facilities would save his life. Anything less would see the death of the founder of Strike Force. Such an eventuality was not to be thought of.

Panting, eyes wild, a figure of despairing, sullen venom, Dolores cowered back among the boulders. Alvilas was not dead. That was the tragedy. She could only hope he would die of his wounds. Die painfully ...

Jorge moved across to her, holding out his hand, and the two Argentinian students sat miserably, awaiting whatever fate these English would mete out.

The fingers moving with such skill to clean and dress the major's wounds, the ice-cold brain directing those fingers, the emotions held under control that would last for as long as was necessary – all these facets of Captain Edward Parkes, R.A.M.C., might just as easily belong to any competent medical man. But for Sawbones, as for the others of Strike Force, the patient represented something far greater even than a single man. The major represented something that each man would have difficulty in explaining. He was the major. He was Strike Force.

Only Tom Burnaby could see a little beyond that immediacy. And what he saw he did not like.

He turned away and bent over Alvilas. The man was unconscious, looking half-dead, and the blood oozed gently. All the members of Strike Force had received medical training, of necessity, and Burnaby got to work. He called out, 'Spider. Give us a pound out, will you.'

Spider came across and together they did for Alvilas what was necessary until Sawbones, assured that he had done all he could for Granville, could take over. He pushed them aside and got on with it. Words were unnecessary.

Going farther along the gully, Burnaby whooshed out a breath. He wiped his forehead and – suddenly and with dramatic intensity – felt the bite of cold all about him.

He saw Smyjo coming up, moving with the uncanny alacrity of a big man. Burnaby looked at Smyjo's face, and saw the rigid set of the jaws, the glisten across the forehead. He braced himself.

'You're back in command, then, Tom.'

'Yes. Look, Smyjo – shouldn't have said that. Forget it, will you?'

'Maybe. But you were right. The girl's a she-cat. I'd no idea – '

Burnaby, about to burst out with something like, 'What the hell did you think I was keeping them apart for?' simply nodded. 'The damage is done. The thing is to get the major to the sub muy pronto. We're moving out right now.'

'Agreed.'

Burnaby took a breath. He faced Smyjo square on. 'Trampas is unfit. He'll go with Sawbones. Jorge and the girl, too. Brax and Smart – '

'What – ?'

'I'm taking two four-man patrols. You and the Whizz

Kid, Ollie and Thwackers in one. Me and Andy, Spider and Lawless in the other.'

'I see.'

'That's right.'

The men of Strike Force did not mince words. A large part of the army used flowery euphemisms. They greased people, for instance. Strike Force said they killed people.

'We're going across to Castillos Field and we're going to mallet them. We are going to take out the super-Exocets. After that we'll go down to the sub.'

'The major said that was a trap, Tom.'

'I know.'

'And you're determined to go?'

'Yes.'

Whilst it was difficult to gauge Smyjo's reactions from what he said and his controlled gestures, Burnaby was suffering from no illusions about the intelligence officer's feelings.

That stiff forefinger brushed across the upper lip. Smyjo spoke quietly. 'Don't you think you'd better speak to the rest of the force?'

'No.'

That was hammering it out, that was nailing it down, that was putting it on the line.

Smyjo leaned back. Burnaby got no satisfaction from the air of unease in the big man, a suggestion that he was nonplussed.

'We're in a hostile country. We're likely to wind up dead. But whilst those Exocets exist, it's our job to take them out.'

'If they exist. Look, Tom – '

'Get the sub party ready, would you, Smyjo? They ought to start moving right away. Anything they can't carry will have to be destroyed. See to it, will you?'

Smyjo favoured him with a look that it was better not to interpret. He nodded.

'Very well.'

When he had gone Burnaby leaned his back against the cold hardness of the rocks and breathed three times with slow deliberateness. The cold came back and then went away. He was himself again.

CHAPTER FOURTEEN

Yomp, said the marines. Tab, said the Paras. The men of Strike Force hacked across that diabolical country, bent under their monstrous burdens, heads jutting, weapons ready, bashing on mile after mile.

Ollie had left his jimpy and now carried the rifle brought in by Andy. They had discarded the bulky wireless set and relied on the pocket Scimitars. Their jaguar packs were stuffed with explosives. Of food they had enough to last them a day and a half, or a day, or two days, depending on whether or not they chose to eat it all at a sitting.

They marched on, beaten by rain, lashed by snow, flailed by winds. Cold was merely a word. It existed. It always had, and probably always would until the big bang engulfed everything. Burnaby's foot where Pugsy had dropped on him hurt. It had to be forced away from his mind. He had to concentrate on going forward, look at the map, check distance and direction, make sure they all kept going. There was no time to dwell on personal miseries. For this there were probably no better troops in the whole damn world. No, that wasn't right. There *were* no better troops in the whole damn world.

Burnaby had set them hacking along, on the trail of the super-Exocets – which might not exist and which might be part of an elaborate trap – without the benefit of a discussion. The conviction that the super-Exocets did exist and must be destroyed obsessed him. Strike Force would go in and do the job for which they had been trained.

After that the recriminations could fly thick and fast. Tom Burnaby wouldn't care.

Had he allowed them the usual discussion on the objectives of their mission, he was dismally convinced that their habitual loyalty to and adoration of Major Granville would have expressed itself in resistance to his plan. The whole atmosphere of this mission would have been different. He would have forced them to obey orders, and they'd have been bloody-minded, understandably so.

As it was, he'd just taken for granted that they'd hack over to Castillos Field. Once they were there and the Exocets were in their sights – malleting time.

If, as the Paras might say, they had to banjo a few folk along the way – too bad. If you jumped with both feet tied together into a war then you could expect to trip up.

It just wasn't true to say, as so many smart-arse commentators did, that most British people didn't know where, who or what the Falklands were until the Argies jumped in with both feet tied together. Anyone with interest in the modern world would know from the television; anyone who had an interest in history would know from Coronel and Graf Spee. Maybe the ties grew fragile over the years, and maybe the kelpers were a bloody-minded lot – with reason – but you had to look at the problems of 1982 with more than a trifle of the outlook that would liken this situation to that of the oafish thief chopping off a tuft of the British lion's tail.

And, just as Burnaby realised the maudlin state of his frame of mind, the thwacketting roar of jet engines hauled him back to reality. Two blurred grey shapes fleeted past above riding the shock waves.

Strike Force did not halt or waver. At that speed and in this murk the pilots would have seen nothing.

When the distant ttick-thrash-tock of helicopter blades rustled down with a shivery menacing beat, Strike Force took stock. They melted. They flowed into cracks and crannies. Counter-surveillance ensured that when the choppers flick-shush-flacked past above, their pilots, too, would see nothing below.

'I'd like to Blowpipe 'em,' announced Spider in a venomous voice.

'And you can carry the bloody thing, too,' Lawless told him, with great satisfaction.

The choppers buzzed away. Burnaby took a breath.

'Castillos Field is three hours away. We can expect company any time.'

He thought of Pugsy. They just had a job to do. They had to do that job. Notions of revenge had no place – in theory. In hot-blooded fact Burnaby was trying to give Pugsy a decent send-off, trying to exorcise the enormous trauma of his death, to dispel the hideous memories of Jock yelling as he was tortured.

The three hours needed to get them to the field would bring them up to the wire with a couple of hours to spare. In that time Burnaby felt they'd be able to prepare themselves. They'd need some breathing space; if they had too much that could so easily work against them. The cold, the isolation, the murk, the feeling that this whole escapade could be a waste of time – or, worse, a cleverly baited trap – might debilitate them. They'd go in because they were Strike Force, trained special soldiers, but they'd go in with the memory of Major Granville's suggestion that it was a trap haunting them. Burnaby wanted them to go in without the spectre of the major hovering over them.

They crossed a lamentable apology for a road and moved steadily up to the field. The settlement lay on the far side, and this they avoided like the plague.

Overlooking Castillos Field they hunkered down and

took stock of the layout. In Spider's jargon, they cased the joint – from a distance.

The French had sold Exocets to Argentina in the normal way of trade in the belief that that fascist country was a part of the West's defence structure. Now that two Western countries were fighting each other, the French had given Britain her full support, proving the staunchest of allies. Details of Exocet and Mirage had been passed to British air intelligence. The French government ordered Aerospatiale to cancel any more Argentinian orders for Exocets and to withhold the team of experts who would have matched the missile to the aircraft. As a result the British thought for a time that the Argies could not launch Exocet from their Super Etendards.

That this was possible had been discovered.

So this fresh batch of super-Exocets – if it existed at all – was not French supplied.

Tom Burnaby lay up overlooking Castillos Field, wondering if the Exocets had been delivered yet, if they had been delayed, if – even – they had arrived, been fitted to aircraft, and were on their way to blow units of the Task Force out of the water around the Falklands.

In a couple of hours, he would lead Strike Force down onto the field and they'd find out.

He called the final O Group – not a Chinese Parliament – and each man thoroughly understood his part in the operation.

'We have no covering or support fire, and we don't really need it,' he told them. He could feel the slow thump of blood in his pulses, the dragging consciousness of imminent failure. These betraying thoughts had to be brushed aside. Easy to say, damned difficult to do …

'This is the most basic kind of op. It's a burn and destroy mission. It's a covert op. We get as far in as we can and do the damage we can before they wake up. Remember: our objectives are the Exocets. If anything else goes up as well, that's a bonus.'

The Whizz Kid smiled.

Smyjo brushed that stiffly military forefinger across his upper lip. 'Ye – es,' he said.

Burnaby eyed him. 'Exocets, Smyjo. I believe they're there, or will be – or have been.'

'If they're there, we'll blow them up.'

'The two patrols go in as two teams. We don't go in from opposite ends. We'll start here – ' he pressed his finger on the map – 'and work along parallel. We want to avoid the slightest chance of shooting one another.'

'Check.'

'Rally point. Well – '

'Go straight on through and out the other side.'

'Only if we hit the Exocets. Otherwise we rally here, at this dispersal point.'

He was fully committed to another sweep if the first failed to turn up the missiles.

'Smyjo. See if you can snaffle an Argie. If we do, we'll run him across to you. We have to get access to information on the latest position.'

The fierce, hairy, grimy, tiger-striped faces bending in that circle of intensely ferocious men would give anyone the shivers. They also were beginning to perfume the air about them. They were, also, damned hungry.

'Oh, surely. We'll ask the questions.' Smyjo radiated the kind of confidence that would pull blood from a stone.

How strange it was, considered Burnaby, that he was perfectly prepared to trust Smyjo with his life, as he would any of the men in Strike Force, yet he couldn't bring himself to like the big guardsman. No, like wasn't the right word. Smyjo had everything going for him. It wasn't liking that was at question here. Rather, it was a generalised feeling of bewilderment at his own instincts, the turmoil of accepted beliefs, the feeling that had life been different he would have made a poor job at being all the things Smyjo represented outside the army and Strike Force.

With each man knowing what he had to do, and with Burnaby's insistence on the importance of what they were about drummed into them – quite unnecessarily, he knew – they could get their heads down for an hour or so.

The O.P. manned by rotation kept up a continual obbo on the field.

Down there they appeared to be sleeping. A few lights showed. This was a field far from danger. That a British force was on the loose on the mainland was now known to the Argies; so far they had failed to detect its presence in the area, or even its line of march after the incidents following the attack on Lobos Field.

Restless, Burnaby sought out Smyjo during his turn at the O.P.

'Look, Smyjo. I understand your feelings and I respect them. But – '

'This isn't necessary, Tom – '

'Listen! This is not your usual hack, burn and run mission. The Exocets ... You'll have to grab an Argie as soon as you can. Nothing blows up until we know what the score is.'

'I understand that.'

Furious with himself, Burnaby went off to get his head down for half an hour.

They'd have to chain the Whizz Kid down, that was for sure ...

On top of everything else he kept on fretting about the rest of Strike Force beetling back to the sub. They wouldn't have an easy time of it either. Well, in this wicked world, who did have an easy time of it – except, perhaps, the wicked?

He did not call Claire Havisham wicked, and she did not have an easy time of it.

The trouble that night had compounded itself in a number of infuriating ways. Paul's Capri proved a comfortable enough ride, and Burnaby felt he could have dozed off. Now it so happened he was wearing a pair of trousers in which the zip, if not pulled to the very top and the tag firmly turned down, had the exasperating habit of running down at every movement. He had dismissed the notion of checking his flies every quarter of an hour or so, mainly on the grounds that this kind of conduct might lead to erroneous if extremely interesting psychological deductions.

So, what with his exertions in the Duck and Drake and lolling on the car seat, and feeling his intrigue with la Havisham's private life growing every moment, the damn zip must have cast off its moorings and pushed out into mid-stream. He was not, of course, aware of it at the time.

He felt more than a little at odds with the world. Claire intrigued him in an understandable use of that much-abused word, and although he was aware that her beauty might unnerve him, he was earthy enough to overcome his first instinctive feelings of distancing.

As the car rounded the corner to halt before the vicarage Burnaby uneasily wondered if there were two completely different Claires.

Paul said he was shaken up by the night's happenings, and intended to drive back to town. He said he was driving back P.D.Q., and that refreshed Burnaby. He smiled.

After the last goodbyes, and Paul's renewed thanks, Burnaby walked up the drive beside Claire. The clinging night-scents of flowers reminded him how lucky people were to live in the country. A shadow at his side in the darkness, Claire walked with that lissomness and swing no beauty parlour could match in a year of ladies' calisthenics. Occasionally her hip brushed against him.

The porch light shone onto the gravel ahead. On the

door, a single glint of brass gleamed from the central knob. The shape of the house was clear against the night sky.

Conversation was not just difficult; it was a downright impossibility. He rasped his tongue around the Sahara cavern of his mouth, and walked along, and realised he was feeling a fool.

The light painted Claire's face. He saw again her sheer beauty. He quelled his automatic fears of distancing. Girls with beauty of that order often bitterly regretted and resented what nature had endowed them with. History was littered with beautiful pathetic wrecks.

The vicar had been pottering in the garden during the day. Burnaby discovered that fact in the next moment.

Claire halted and turned to him, smiling, her head up.

'You have been very kind – Tom. I don't think Paul would have – '

Burnaby, moving on and sideways to accommodate his movements to her abrupt halt, tripped over the vicar's abandoned rake. The haft whistled up and struck him in the back, a sharp blow all along his spine.

He whooped a startled exclamation, got his feet tangled, and toppled forward, hands reaching out instinctively.

He lunged full into Claire. His grasping hands, seeking some secure hold, fastened upon round, soft protuberances. He scrabbled for support, almost falling, gripping on. He leaned on her, tilting her back, and she stood for a heart-beat unmoving.

Then – and he admired it in the instant he felt her hand on him – she twisted sideways and clouted him over the head. He got the vicar's damn broom between his legs and fell down. On his back, looking up, he saw her silhouette against the porch light above him.

Her voice was penetrating, even and hard.

'Goodnight, Mr Burnaby.'

'But – Claire – I didn't – it was this – '

'I have nothing to say to you. Except that just because a girl takes her clothes off to make a living does not give you the excuse to treat her as a common slut.'

'Claire!'

'And cover yourself up.'

'Do what?'

He looked down in panic. That God-forsaken zip! Pure white Y-fronts gleamed with leering anticipation in the glow of the porch light.

When he looked up she was just opening the door. It slammed like a 155mm. howitzer going off in his ear. He let out a puff of air. The night closed in, soft and romantic and sweetly scented. And when he sat up and grasped the zip to haul it up he discovered the confounded thing was jammed down. So, of course, all he could do was laugh. No other reaction would have made sense in that situation.

CHAPTER FIFTEEN

The next morning, wearing a different pair of trousers, he'd gone round to the vicarage. He could explain it all, reasonably enough. The rake and the broom stood leaning against the porch wall, inoffensive gardening implements. Last night they'd been the weapons of the devil.

The vicar's housekeeper said that Miss Havisham had gone back to London. Early. There was no message.

So, here he was, overlooking Castillos Field, about to go down and strew mayhem and destruction, and try to prevent the possible deaths of many men in the Task Force off the Falklands, with the thought of Miss Claire Havisham burning in his brain – for that had been only one of their early encounters. What had followed had burned other areas of his body beside his brains.

The Whizz Kid went past looking his usual evil self, Spider hunkered down beside Burnaby, and Lawless roused himself and sat up. Instantly, Burnaby sensed a ganging-up on him.

Spider said, 'Andy's on obbo now, Tom. When we go down there – '

'Yes,' said Burnaby.

Lawless, in his pragmatic, mechanic's way, tried, too.

'If you go too fast, don't expect me to keep up with you.'

'We'll be in contact.'

'Somebody has to – ' and then Lawless stopped himself

from saying any more. The memory of Pugsy and Jock aroused feelings that could not be put into words.

Then it was time.

On the way down Burnaby allowed himself to luxuriate in the feeling of comradely purpose; here he was with a fine, ferocious bunch of comrades marching into danger. Then he banished those unreal, romantic thoughts and let himself get into the real business of Strike Force.

The perimeter of the field presented no real obstacle. The two four-man patrols eased along cautiously and silently. It was just murky enough to conceal their movements. Objects tended to appear with suddenness and a man could find himself on top of an obstacle where a moment before nothing showed ahead. They prowled. They were hunting trouble. God help anyone who tried to stop them ...

They were going in without a fire base to afford support and whilst this might go against the grain, in this situation covering fire would have been so problematical as to have been nearly valueless. Here it would be a question of man versus man.

The first Argie Burnaby came across was having a quiet spit and draw hunkered beside a pile of oil drums. His eyes almost fell out of his head when he saw the two evil-looking men, all hair and grime, tiger-striped faces and monstrous humped packs, looming over him. Their rifles prodded his stomach and the cigarette fell from his mouth.

Andy put his foot on it.

'Grab him. Let's run him across to Smyjo – '

'No kill me,' quavered the Argentinian. He fell down in a paroxysm of fear, so abruptly generated he had no time to find his courage. These men pounced with diabolical swiftness.

'Speak English?' said Andy in his conversational voice, which might have melted steel at ten paces.

'No. No. No kill me.' The Argie writhed like a cat before the fire. 'Friend. No kill me.'

'Hit him over the head,' suggested Andy.

'Better tie him up. Don't want to damage the merchandise.'

'Right.'

They used his own belts to effect this and then Andy eyed the man's boots. Argentine army boots were vastly superior to British issue, as they'd rapidly found out.

'No time, Andy. We can come back for them.'

'Right.'

Gagged and bound, the Argentinian was hauled along. Smyjo would have to talk to him. His general attitude did not indicate the elite forces Burnaby had expected to find. If the field was guarded by conscripts, the task would be a trifle easier. Just a trifle.

Flanked by the other patrol, the line of advance led past marker beacons, the side of the strip, and a couple of parked aircraft. Their indistinct silhouettes gave Burnaby the impression they were twin-engined civil craft, but he did not stop to investigate. They were not Super Etendards. They would not carry and launch Exocets against the Task Force.

They pressed on, warily. The sheds which were objective number one showed as a series of peaks. Burnaby hunkered down, watching, as Andy hauled the prisoner to the ground. The silence provided a comforting shroud they did not wish to dissolve.

Spider and Lawless reported no sign of Super Etendards or Exocets on their axis. Burnaby used his pocket Scimitar and called Smyjo.

'We have a mark one for you.'

'Right.'

Burnaby, impressed by the marvels and mysteries of science, hauled the Argentinian close. He shoved the pocket Scimitar at the man's head, twisted his head to speak.

'Go ahead. Listening.'

From the tiny radio Smyjo's voice rattled off rapid Spanish. The prisoner looked shocked. He jerked back. Andy held him as a butcher holds the pig's head on the block, cleaver raised.

Presently the man managed to stutter out something, gobbling his words, the gag dangling under his chin. If he shouted now ... Andy made very clear what would happen to him if he was so foolish ...

Smyjo's voice over the set said, 'You've caught a throw-back minnow there. The man's an imbecile. He knows nothing.'

'Or says he knows nothing,' said Andy in a voice like barbed wire.

Once again Smyjo tried, and when the quick flow of Spanish ceased, said, 'No go. We have to find ourselves somebody with at least two O Levels.'

'Right. Out,' and Burnaby stashed the radio.

'Tie him up good, Andy. We try again.'

After all, what more could you expect? Some miserable little conscript, shivering on guard duty, taking a surreptitious drag at his cigarette – what would he know of the presence or otherwise of top-secret military hardware?

'If there are mechanics working in the hangars,' he told Andy. 'They might know. Or the damned missiles might be there.'

'Let's go.'

The murk covered their approach to the hangars. A crack of light shafted lemon-yellow radiance onto the concrete. Andy, like a lethal shadow of destruction, moved ahead. Burnaby prepared himself for more nastiness.

These poor damned Argies. And this bloody silly war. All for a few lumps of rock. All right, the junta had tried to bolster their own regime and its innate incompetence by foreign adventure, the oldest ploy in the political book. And, all right, so the Falklands were so British as to admit of no valid counter-argument, no matter how much squawk went up from South America. The British Government had vacillated – which was for them a usual ploy, too – only this time the fuse had burned down before they'd expected. If the Falklands were, in the end, handed over to Argentina, Burnaby did not think anyone would be vastly surprised.

The shades of the dead lads, and their relatives, might wonder about it all, though ...

He was a soldier, and he had been given instructions; as he pushed open the little access door in the larger hangar door, he had to banish all his political doubts. Of course he was scared stiff, but that wasn't a part of this parcel of doubts nagging at him.

Four men in mechanic's overalls sat around a packing crate playing cards. A pool of mellow light enveloped them, isolating their group from the shadows of the hangar. Dots of light here and there along the overhead splashed onto the outlines of aircraft. The warm smell of oil and grease brisked up the goose pimples after the bitter outside air.

The aircraft were Skyhawks – A4Q/P probably – and Burnaby decided they'd have to be destroyed in due time. The men playing cards, engrossed in their game, huddled in mutual comradeship and gamesmanship, were aware of nothing. A couple of rifles propped against a barrel to one side had to be figured into the equation. Burnaby nodded at Andy, and the two Strike Force men went in.

The deal had just been completed, and the mechanics studied their hands. One, rolling his eyes heavenwards and, no doubt, about to indulge in some histrionics about the evils of fate and the diabolical hand he'd been dealt, saw Andy.

His rolling eyes became transfixed. His mouth dropped

open. He emitted a gargling squeak and the cards fluttered from his fingers. The fellow at his side, nearest the rifles, swivelled. He wore chevrons. He did not hesitate. He snatched up a rifle and levelled it. Andy was beaten for speed only by Burnaby.

The knife flew from Burnaby's fingers in a silver liquid gleam. It penetrated the mechanic's throat, smashing in a chunking razor-sharp throw that ripped Adam's Apple, tendons, veins, that drove the man back off his stool and threw him sprawling onto the oil-stained floor.

Andy's rifle switched from one to the other of the three remaining.

He barked out, 'Silencio!' which, correct or not, had the desired effect.

Burnaby walked towards the packing crate, his rifle now held firmly. It did not tremble. He looked fierce, deliberately fierce, and the men shrank back.

He looked down at the cards.

'He didn't have aces and eights, Andy. But it would have fitted.'

Burnaby kicked the fallen rifle away. The three mechanics, shrunken, remained petrified.

Andy came over and took the other rifle out of temptation's reach. He looked with a low, brooding stare on the Argentinians. What they were thinking about the two men from Strike Force God alone knew.

That particular knife had been a favourite of Burnaby's for some time. It flew with a perfect balance and he could split a fly in half at twenty paces. Or so he said, with a smile. He bent and did the necessary and messy things required to pull a knife from a dead man's throat. He got no blood on his boot. He'd started off calling that knife Betsy, then he'd decided that was too childish, smacking of juvenile romanticism. The knife killed people before they killed him or his friends.

He wiped it carefully, and as the cloth caressed the blade and brought the steel back to shining silver, so he let his eyes open and stare meaningfully upon the three mechanics.

Andy well understood the theatrical business.

'If they know, they'll talk,' he said, and took out his Scimitar.

Before he could call out an explosion thumped dully from outside. The wall of the hangar shook, the lights flickered madly and dust sifted down. The three mechanics just dived flat on the floor, hands over their heads.

Another explosion smashed in, and the doors flew open. An enormous rage filled Burnaby. 'Goddammit! If that's the Whizz Kid I'll castrate the lunatic!' He ran for the door.

Two men ran inside, yelling. They wore the bulky Argentinian helmets, and Burnaby just slugged them and leaped over their falling bodies.

Outside, the field jumped with fresh explosions. The detonations sounded crisper in the open, unmuffled by hangar walls. Sheets of flame rose from the far side of the strip. That was where they'd marked down one ammunition dump. Perhaps ... ?

His Scimitar failed to respond when he called out. What the hell was going on?

The flames roared up, twisting and writhing. Andy appeared at his side, a mechanic clutched in each fist, dragged along like potato sacks.

'That's not ammo, Tom. That's fuel.'

'Right. No one's answering on the radio.'

A shadow moved beside the wall and in the instant Burnaby's rifle twitched in that direction, a Cockney voice yelped, 'Strike! Spider!'

They trotted up, Spider and Lawless, together.

'What the hell's going on?'

'How do I know? Find any Exocets?'

'Not a one. Been all along the axis. Ollie and Thwackers had a no result on their side.'

'So it's Smyjo and the Whizz Kid. I might have known.'

The crashing succession of explosions quietened down to a steady roaring as the fuel burned. The flames lit the undersides of black clouds, obscuring everything, smoke wafting away on the wind. The heat was just noticeable at this distance.

A series of rectangles of light sprang into being in the air off to the side.

'That's the tower catching on.'

Burnaby bellowed into the Scimitar.

'Smyjo! Where the hell are you, Smyjo!'

'It's a monumental cock-up,' pronounced Andy.

Abrupt and treacherous doubt hit Burnaby. Was Andy suggesting that had the major been here the mission would have been a success? Or– perhaps worse still – that there were no super-Exocets at all and the major had said so and wouldn't have brought the lads here?

He lifted the radio and felt the desperation in him.

'Smyjo! Come in, Smyjo! Where the hell are you?'

'Right here, old boy,' came Smyjo's voice from the corner of the hangar.

Burnaby whirled.

Smyjo and the Whizz Kid walked in. Had their faces not been tiger-striped they'd have been as black as soot. Some of the Whizz Kid's hair was distinctly singed.

Instantly, Burnaby was in control of himself.

'What happened?'

'No idea.' Smyjo passed that military forefinger across his upper lip. 'The Whizz Kid was laying charges, all strictly according to the book. One of 'em must have been duff. Anyway, the whole kaboodle went off. I must say we were lucky to get away.'

'Yes. Good. Couple of Argies for you. Mechanics. They'll know – '

'Right. Get on it straightaway.'

A certain aura of guilt hung about Smyjo. Burnaby could take scant comfort from that. He tilted his head and stared at the lights shining from the tower windows. The Argies would be responding in no time flat now ...

Once they knew where the super-Exocets were hidden Strike Force would have to go in like G.F.L. 'Gee-eff-ell,' as the men said. In other words, go in like greased lightning.

Smyjo was gabbling away to the Argies suspended from Andy's massive fists. He bent his head, thrusting his face forward like a bird of prey. He did not touch the Argentinians.

He swung about abruptly, lifting his hands and then allowing them to swing down to his sides, with a controlled gesture. He marched up to Burnaby. The others crowded close.

'It's no go, Tom. Those mechs were here for the Exocets – '

'So they do exist!'

'Too right. But they're not here yet. They're being brought in with a strong Argentine Special Forces guard.'

'What?'

'That's the picture, my old son. They're being flown in. We've struck a day too early.'

Across Castillos Field the burning fuel dump roared and belched away, lurid streaks of light brightening the murky sky. The rumble of engines sounded close by and the thin wail of a ghostlike alarm siren cut through the racket. Somewhere some idiot let loose a full clip. Strike Force was sitting squarely in the middle of what amounted to an enraged beehive. In moments the Argentinians would move in, shooting …

'Tomorrow.' Burnaby didn't know how he felt.

'As I commented,' said Andy. 'A monumental cock-up.'

CHAPTER SIXTEEN

Tom Burnaby damn well *did* know how he felt. He felt so savage a determination swamp him that all emotions of rage vanished. He was icily calm.

'So they're flying in tomorrow. And they have Special Forces. All right. We'll still take the bastards out.'

Flames scattered lurid reflections across the edge of the hangars. A drop of firelight caught in Burnaby's eye, and gleamed like blood.

He was an only child, and consequently had not had the sibling experience of struggling for recognition and getting his own way from square one. He had had to learn the hard way how to trample over other people; it was not natural to him. Now he glared balefully around upon the men of Strike Force, those that were left, his gaze meaningful. Captain Tom Burnaby, a soldier, stiffened his spine and told his men what they were going to do.

'That plane bringing the Exocets in is never going to land here when the pilot sees what's going on. That fuel will burn right through past dawn. So we take the tower and convince the pilot the trouble is just a local spot of bother – an accident. Smyjo – that's your job.'

'The pilot will probably know the traffic controller's voice – '

'So you convince the traffic controller!'

Smyjo did not brush his finger across his upper lip. But his head went up.

'They're pushing in a trifle, Tom,' called Spider from just past the corner of the hangar.

'Right. We move out now. Left and right axis. Just keep going. Anybody gets in the way – too bad. But save this famous traffic controller for Smyjo.'

'Check.'

He used his radio and this time raised Thwackers and Ollie. He simply told them what they had to do, and cut the switch.

They moved out towards the tower.

Burnaby did not feel inclined to think of these men as a desperate bunch. They were in a tight spot, yes. They were surrounded by hostiles, and they had to do a job that might get them all killed. But, all the same, they were still Strike Force. That still counted.

A 30 mm. auto-cannon opened up from the tower roof. The shells struck furrows along the ground past the hangars.

'Some clever bastard up there with a nightsight,' growled Andy. No one bothered to shoot back. They ran for the cover of a helicopter parked on the near side of the apron. The Argentine gunner had too much respect for property to shoot at them behind the chopper. Looking around past the tail rotor, Burnaby spotted the line of advancing men.

They looked like a frieze of black felt, like cut-outs, like – God forgive him – like targets in a shooting gallery.

Andy said, 'Like going over the top in Kaiser Bill's war.'

'We'll have to see them off before we break through.'

The men of Strike Force settled down to application.

As the advancing soldiers began to drop, their advance slowed, faltered, stopped. They ran for cover. A last few final rounds convinced them of the wisdom of their choice.

'Now,' observed Smyjo, 'we have to do the same.'

'Let Thwackers and Ollie do their stuff first.'

A quick trigger-call over the Scimitar resulted in the concussive explosions of grenades. Ollie and Thwackers lobbed them in with abandon.

'Go!'

The six men picked themselves up and fairly hurled themselves on. Disoriented by the sudden crish-crash of grenades falling on them from an unexpected direction, the Argentine military remained fast in their positions. It was a fine old race, a touch and go business, and at the end a few shots spurted at the heels of Burnaby, who felt the blood in him fairly boiling with effort.

He landed in a heap under the tower steps. A shadow appeared above him and Spider shot the shadow away. The noise blended into a pandemonium of shots and yells and the crackling roar of the conflagration hammering unendingly over all.

Up the steps. A figure at the door. Trigger him and go on – go on!

In the door. More soldiers. The blaze and blaze of sub-machine gun fire, the feel of bullets tugging at his sleeve. The rifle in his hands spewed tumble-bullets, strewing death. Men toppled, glass smashed, the stink of fumes stifled. Blood splashed.

When it was all over the men of Strike Force gazed about on a shambles.

'Spider. Drop grenades on 'em if they try to get up the steps.'

Spider shot twice, methodically, out into the flame-lit darkness, before acknowledging.

The Argentine Smyjo selected as the senior traffic controller sat cowering in his chair, his hands over his face. Blood streaked the back of his left hand.

In a voice that he might have used to wheedle a pet collie, Smyjo spoke in his beautiful Spanish.

The man did not respond. Smyjo tried again.

Ollie said, 'I think ... ' and fell down.

Instantly, Burnaby leaped across, catching the limp body as Ollie toppled. He felt the blood along Ollie's side.

He looked up.

'He's taken one in his side. Thwackers, patch him up.'

Without speaking, Thwackers ripped out his kit and prepared to tend his wounded comrade. If Ollie could be saved by them, he would be. Burnaby went back to the radio equipment.

'It all seems okay. Lawless, see what you can find at the back. Anything been shot away.'

The Signals people got on with their job. Smyjo went on cajoling the Argentinian survivor. His own comrades still lay where they had fallen, sprawled in their own blood. The Whizz Kid began to place his nasty little packages in strategic places, ready for the off.

Spider watched the stairs.

Andy climbed the ladder to the roof, and returned quickly after a burst of gunfire.

'Pushed 'em off the edge. Less messy.'

'Everything's working. Now it's up to Smyjo and the traffic controller.'

The big guardsman looked around.

'He's still in shock. I may have to try to talk to the aircraft pilot myself.'

'You'll be all right.'

'It's a chance – '

'What bloody-well isn't?'

Spider moved twice.

From outside the crunch of two grenades was followed by screams.

'Only two more.'

'Divvy up,' ordered Burnaby.

Andy collected the grenades. He placed them beside the door. The fight had blown out a majority of the bulbs; the remaining few flickered and then died.

'Now why should they cut that power?' said Burnaby. 'The tower has its own generator – anybody knows that.'

Spider said, 'They're getting restless out there.' A pause. Then, 'The cunning bastards. They're bringing up a damned great cannon.'

Burnaby was at the door.

He used his nightsight.

It was probably an ancient anti-tank gun, left over from the Second World War, but it would punch nasty great holes in the tower and if the shells hit anyone they would punch nasty holes through them.

'See if you can pick 'em off, Spider. Lawless, get over here.'

The Light Support Weapon team crouched low. Spider lined up. Burnaby had to leave them to it as Smyjo called.

'Well?'

'I've fed him pills. He's coherent now. I think he'll do it.'

Burnaby eyed the traffic controller, seeing his thin olive-brown face, the moustache black and drooping a little now, the ravaged lines around his eyes and mouth. He looked scared clean through, brickless, as the lads said.

'It can't be long now.' As he spoke Spider opened up. The burst was short and accurate. In reply a volley of shots broke in through the tower windows. At the angle from which they were fired they punched up on to the ceiling. 'Just keep him up to snuff.'

A yell from Spider informed those interested that he had knocked over the damned gunner. Whatever he had done, the anti-tank gun did not fire.

A lightening of the murk beyond the smashed windows heartened Burnaby. So far it had been easy. No resolute counter-attack had been put in. At this rate, they could hold on till Doomsday.

Then a mortar bomb hit the roof and brought a cascade

of debris down on their heads.

Burnaby's chief concern was for the radio equipment. Through the smoke and dust he fought across to the control board. The traffic controller was on his face under the desk, hands over his head. Smyjo hoisted him up.

Another bomb exploded off to the side.

'Any sign!' bellowed Burnaby.

'Nothing. Got to be just beyond the hangars.'

There was no way they were going to take out the mortar from here. Burnaby began the sickening selection in his head. Who should go. Who could he spare.

Thwackers came over, coughing.

'Ollie's okay. I'll go.'

'Hold it, Thwackers ... '

Distantly, was that the sound of jet engines?

'Get your friend up, Smyjo. In his chair. Call out.'

Smyjo responded with alacrity and the traffic controller was lifted bodily and dumped before the console. He had recovered himself, no doubt because of Smyjo's pills, and now he began to call out.

The answer sputtered in, and Burnaby flicked on the speaker.

The traffic controller spoke rapidly, and then turned to look at Smyjo. The speaker continued to rattle with the pilot's voice.

Smyjo said, 'He says he can't get through. The set's smashed.'

'Is that so?' Burnaby looked with more interest at the Argentinian traffic controller. The fellow was trying, then. It had all been a little too much for him, what with these hairy, tiger-striped maniacs bursting in shooting. Death and blood and destruction everywhere about him ... But he was trying. Good on yer, sport, said Burnaby to himself, and leaned forward and did the necessary things that cut in the correct radio circuits.

'Tell him I'm a signals buff. He won't fool me.'

With that the brief resistance of the traffic controller ceased – for now.

The light brightened. Burnaby tried to envisage the scene on Castillos Field as the incoming pilot would see it. There was a lot of smoke and flame from the fuel dump. There were no smashed aircraft. He wouldn't be able to see the broken windows in the tower. If Smyjo convinced the tough little Argie to speak his proper lines it would work. It had to work. It damned well had to!

A fresh flurry of shots, punching up into the tower, heralded a fresh attack. This time the grenades halted it dead, Spider shot off another mag, and the attack died back.

'Two grenades left,' announced Andy.

'One mag – '

'Here, Lawless. Take my mags.' Burnaby handed his rifle mags across. They'd spew from the Light Support Weapon, and then there would be none left. By that time, the aircraft must be a charred wreck. Had to be. The people and vessels of the Task Force might be charred wrecks if Strike Force failed here.

The pilot's voice sounded, even to the listening English ears, highly dubious. The traffic controller rattled off what Smyjo told him to say – there had been an unfortunate accident and a fuel dump had caught fire. But there was nothing to stop the Boeing from landing safely.

The tension of those moments carried as much emotional punch as everything that had gone before. This was tantalizing. If that damned Boeing pilot smelled a rat, and winged away …

The aircraft was a civvy job on charter to the naval authorities. The pilot would be more chary than otherwise. Sweating it out, Burnaby stared through the gaping windows. The shape of the plane showed, monstrous in the misty light, winging down. He began to breathe out a shaky sigh when the traffic controller burst into a torrent of words.

Smyjo hit him over the head, dragged him away from the microphone, started to rattle off his own faultless Spanish.

No one needed to spell the score. Burnaby spared a single scarlet thought for the little Argentinian traffic controller, a tough, brave little bastard, and then he was staring mesmerised at the Boeing.

The Argies down on the field had lit a bonfire on the runway. If that didn't warn the pilot, the frantic warning over his radio must ...

Spider loosed off again, and screams and the thump of men falling down the stairs, the smash of the penultimate grenade, told Burnaby his time was up. So there was only one thing to do.

He went up the ladder to the roof like a powder monkey up the ratlines of a seventy-four. The Boeing was on an approach course to the runway, drawing closer with fiendish speed. Bullets began to crack about his ears. He ignored them. He grabbed the 30 mm. auto-cannon, swung the muzzle around. He lined up the antique cross wires and circle sights, got the sleek outlines of the civil Boeing square. He allowed for the speed, and pressed the trigger.

The 30 mm. shells began to spew out.

He'd no idea how many rounds were left. He just held the trigger down and swung the gun and allowed his instinctive sighting reflexes to take over. He was not aware of his shells striking.

Then Smyjo screamed in his ear. 'You're hitting him! Good shooting, Tom!'

Smoke licked back evilly from the nearest outboard engine.

A touch of elevation, swing with the gun as the big Boeing thundered past, keep the trigger down, shudder as the gun shoots … He saw the blister of aluminium shards from around the pilot's cabin. The Boeing went rushing on. The gun hammered dead with a last dry click.

The Boeing bored on, lifting, turning to climb safely away.

The engine snorted smoke and burst into flame.

The plane turned slowly, majestically, like a wounded beast. Then, with a suddenness that took the breath away, it turned over, dived and smashed into the ground. An enormous boil of orange and black vomited up, and when the noise racketted in it drowned the sullen crackle from the fuel dump, blotting out everything else.

Smyjo's hand on his shoulder. Smyjo's voice in his ear like a thin screech of a fingernail on glass – something to do with well done, and that's done it.

Tiredness had to be pushed away before it destroyed him.

Spider bellowed up. 'They're coming in again!'

Burnaby had himself together. He jumped down the ladder followed by Smyjo. He glared about.

'Thwackers – grab Ollie. We're leaving – '

'I can make it on my tod,' said Ollie, with a flash of spirit.

'Hit 'em with the last grenade, then down and off. Make for that chopper. Shoot all the way. And don't any of you get hit.'

The Whizz Kid did what was necessary with his infernal devices. He spoke. 'Seventy-five seconds.'

'Let's go!'

The grenade span away. They leaped down the ladder, and Burnaby heaved the unconscious form of the traffic controller out and down to where he would be out of the coming blast effect. They heard the crack of bullets. They shot at the bulbous-helmeted heads of the Argies. Bullets kicked into the ground about them. Burnaby felt them stitching at his sleeves. He ran on, shooting. Everyone was shooting.

Into the helicopter, with Andy and Smyjo and Spider and Lawless and Ollie and Thwackers shooting back, a massive concentration of fire power. The noise was stupendous. He understood the controls of the helicopter perfectly, for Strike Force trained its people well. Pity Noggy wasn't here at the controls, instead of falling off a damned sub; but he wasn't and Burnaby got the motor going and the vanes turning. He felt not so much detached as interested from a distance in what he was doing, what the others were doing, how the chopper reacted. It was akin to an exercise with real bullets and real blood and real death.

The helicopter lifted.

She lifted and Burnaby swung her low and felt himself as a part of the machine. He took her slicing past the hangars and Andy was still shooting down from the open door. The chopper swooped away, leaving the twin palls of smoke, leaving the pyre that was the incineration of super-Exocets.

Now they had a quick run to the coast, sharp and no nonsense, where they'd radio the sub. After that – well, what happened then would be another mission for Strike Force.

The whole of Castillos Field appeared to be burning. The fuel dump, the tower, the hangars where the Whizz Kid's infernal devices were brewing up Skyhawks, and the grotesque tangle that had once been Exocets to destroy the British Task Force, all burned.

No one in the great outside world would ever hear of this. Of course not. Pugsy, Jock – they would appear as lamentable deaths in some part of the Falklands Campaign.

The helicopter sped for the coast buzzing like a hornet. Burnaby wondered about Major Dan Granville and what the future held for their relationship. It would probably be barbed and prickly and unpleasant – and Burnaby could not find an atom of triumph in the knowledge that he had been right.

Strike Force had been called in to do this job, to carry out Mission Exocet. This they had done. Now they could go back to what they'd been called away from – going ashore in the Falklands and creating merry hell.

Thinking of that, Burnaby thought of Claire Havisham and how they'd parted in the end – he'd sort all that nonsense out as soon as he got back. But, first – the Falklands ...